"You can't
Elaine protested

"Oh, I'm serious, all right. Absolutely. You once told me," Guy reminded her, "that the most important ingredient for marriage is compatibility. And compatibility is something we do have. Think about your life-style and mine. It could work very well, indeed."

Elaine stared at him. He was proposing marriage. How could he be so calm, so cool?

"Don't say anything now. Think about it," he added.

She didn't have to think it over. She wanted to say yes. Yes, yes, yes! But that wasn't what she was going to say. She was going to refuse.

There was no way she would agree to marry a man who didn't love her. What about her theories, the ones she'd had before she knew how she felt about Guy? They still held, didn't they?

Claudia Jameson lives in Berkshire, England, with her husband and family. She is an extremely popular author in both the Harlequin Presents and Harlequin Romance series. And no wonder! Her lively dialogue and ingenious plots—with the occasional dash of suspense—make her a favorite with romance readers everywhere.

Books by Claudia Jameson

Don't miss any of our special offers. Write to us at the following address for information on our newest releases.

Harlequin Reader Service
901 Fuhrmann Blvd., P.O. Box 1397, Buffalo, NY 14240
Canadian address: P.O. Box 603,
Fort Erie, Ont. L2A 5X3

A Man of Contrasts

Claudia Jameson

Harlequin Books

TORONTO • NEW YORK • LONDON
AMSTERDAM • PARIS • SYDNEY • HAMBURG
STOCKHOLM • ATHENS • TOKYO • MILAN

Original hardcover edition published in 1987
by Mills & Boon Limited

ISBN 0-373-02857-1

Harlequin Romance first edition September 1987

Printed in U.S.A.

CHAPTER ONE

ELAINE paused to look at the photograph given prominence in the display in the window of Faraday & Faraday, Estate Agents. The house was not particularly big, was hardly spectacular, but it had once been her home. For the moment it still was. Her eyes shifted to the asking price beneath the photo. The turnover of houses in North Manchester was very slow at the moment. There was a lot of unemployment in the area and apart from that, people were away on holiday; it might be months before a buyer turned up. Well, she would be prepared to drop the price if necessary, not that she was in any hurry to get rid of the place.

To get rid of the place. The words made her shiver in spite of the brilliant July sunshine. It had been only a week ago that she had been able to take any action, make a decision on what to do about her parents' house . . . what had been her parents' house. Prior to that she had been in shock, in a mental fog which was only just lifting. Even now, she was in a state of nervous tension. It was hardly surprising. The horror of her parents' death was going to take much longer than six months to adjust to.

She caught sight of her own reflection in the window, her black hair hanging symmetrically in its trouble-free cut. A parting down the centre, a heavy fringe, the rest silky and straight, almost touching her shoulders. Unfashionable, perhaps, but what did she care about fashion? Her hand came up to touch the floppy tie around the neck of her blouse. The tie was fashionable, at least. Navy skirt, navy tie, white blouse—she felt as if she were in school uniform. But one could hardly conduct business as an estate agent in jeans, tee-shirt and sandals, which was the way she preferred to be dressed. She had had to buy a few new outfits to wear for this kind of work.

The young receptionist greeted her as she stepped inside the offices. 'Nice lunch, Miss Faraday?'

Elaine nodded, smiled, and was walking straight through to her office as Pamela went on.

'There were two messages for you. Mr Brahmin phoned, he's very interested in the flat he saw in Whitefield this morning, wants you to ring him back. The other call was from your . . . your father's solicitor. He'll call you back.'

There was always a pause, a shifting of eyes, when Elaine's father was mentioned. Pamela had worked for him for a year prior to the plane crash which killed him. Him and Elaine's mother. And several other members of her family, almost an entire family wiped out in one appalling tragedy which had shocked the country, probably the whole world.

'Thanks, Pam.' Elaine never remembered to ask about messages, she always had to be told. It was either the effect of her perpetual preoccupation or simply because she was not business-orientated. Or both. Her own small business, which had been neglected these past six months, did not involve any pressure, any complications, in fact, she didn't even think of it as a business. To her it was just a living, a living earned in a way that gave her enormous pleasure. There was nothing she would rather do. If she were to learn and carry on her father's business she would make much more money, but money was not her main priority in life, and anyway, she simply wasn't a businesswoman Still, Pamela never showed any sign of impatience. She had been wonderfully supportive and helpful through these difficult months. Elaine had asked Pamela to address her by her first name, but she never did. She seemed to think some distance had to be kept between a receptionist and the boss's daughter—or rather, the boss. Elaine was in control of her father's business now; it was hers, lock, stock and problems, the major problem being how to dispose of it. And to whom?

She went into the office which had been her father's, sat behind his desk, and looked at the photograph of him and his wife, framed and perched on a corner. It had been there for years. They were both in their early thirties in the photo. Her eyes closed as a stab of pain shot through her. They had been only in their middle forties when they had died . . .

'Sorry to interrupt.' Her eyes flew open as Don Black knocked once, briefly, at the door. He swept into the office in his usual energetic, swift-moving fashion and sat down. 'Are you all right, Elaine?'

'Yes. You're not interrupting, Don. I—was just thinking.'

He was frowning, though. 'Try not to, love. Not about that, anyway. Elaine, why do you insist on being such a loner? Why did you take off for lunch without telling me? I was free, I could have gone with you.' His impatient tone dropped suddenly, he tried to laugh it off. 'I mean, you should have grabbed me while you had the chance!'

She smiled. Don Black was a nice man. A childless divorcee, he was in his late twenties, and had worked for her father for three years. Dad had been thinking of making him a partner, had spoken about it only a short time before taking that fateful flight. Did Don know this? She supposed not. John Faraday would have thought it through before saying anything to his employee. That had been his nature, to think things over carefully before acting.

Elaine's father had never made a wrong business move in his life. At least, if he had she didn't know about it. Not that she had ever shown any particular interest in his business. Faraday & Faraday, established over fifty years, had been started by her paternal grandfather; John Faraday had joined the business straight after leaving school, hence the name. He had had sole control since Grandad's death eight years earlier, Elaine remembered.

Don Black was manager now; he had been concerned chiefly with commercial properties rather than domestic ones but at the moment he was overseeing every transaction which took place in the business. He had to: Elaine couldn't. Oh, she was there, doing her best at pretending to be an estate agent, for the time being. But she would soon have another decision to make. She had put the house up for sale, and soon the business would have to go, too. There was another alternative open to her, but Don wanted the business, he had told her that; the trouble was that he had no money to speak of. He had suggested a deal which sounded highly complicated to Elaine, the details of which she'd forgotten except that it would result in her having an income from the business instead of a lump sum from an outright sale. She was only just beginning to think clearly and so had not yet asked him to go over his proposal again.

Whatever happened, she was grateful to him for his help and support these past months. She had told him so more than once. Don had put up with a lot during that time: her bursting into tears, her confusion, bewilderment, inefficiency. 'I see you've put the photo of *Rosalie* in the window,' she said now,

'Just—while you were out. It looks good, doesn't it? You checked through the details again before they were duplicated, I hope?'

She had. 'Three bedrooms, one with bathroom en suite. Second bathroom. Fourth bedroom or study on the ground floor. Large fitted kitchen/breakfast room. Living room with French windows leading on to patio. Separate dining room. Utility room and downstairs toilet. Gas central heating. Gardens, two-thirds of an acre.'

It was a nice house with pleasant views, situated in Tottington, just north-east of Bury, where the estate agency was, and it had been easy for her father to commute between home and work. 'Rosalie' had been her mother's name.

'Elaine?'

'Sorry, I was——'

'Just thinking—I know. Look, you've got to stop dwelling on things. Let me take you out for a meal tonight, take your mind off your worries.'

'No, thanks all the same.' She smiled to soften her refusal. Don had asked her out several times lately. She honestly didn't know whether he fancied her or whether he was merely being kind. Or maybe he wanted to befriend her so she would agree to his taking over the business. Or all three.

At twenty-two Elaine had had her fair share of boyfriends, though none for the past two years, almost two years. None of them had been serious and she was certainly not on the lookout. She could take them or leave them, was perfectly content living alone and doing her own thing. She loved her work. And there was nothing wrong with being a loner, to use Don's word. It was different from being lonely; she was never lonely—but then again, her family had always been there, available whenever she wanted to see them. Now—well, she might learn what loneliness meant in the future. She had been left with only one cousin, and he lived in London.

'Would you mind telling me why?' Don was watching her, his curiosity apparent.

'Because it's Friday and I'm going home tonight. I mean home to my own place. I have to check that everything's okay.'

'In the middle of the Yorkshire Dales, what do you

suppose could go wrong?'

'The Lancashire Moors,' she corrected. Elaine's home was in the Forest of Bowland, a picturesque and beautiful spot which was, to her, paradise. The nearest neighbours to her cottage were a mile away, the tranquillity not only a source of pleasure but also conducive to the exacting work she did. Around her cottage were neat little gardens she tended herself, a job she loved, and its background was of hills, open countryside which soothed her spirit. 'Home' was almost two hours' drive from Bury, which was why she was living temporarily in her parents' house. Until she—yes, until she got rid of it. True, it held only happy memories for her but it was of no use to her now. Her parents were *gone*. She simply had to adjust to that fact.

'Don, about the house—I mean *Rosalie*—do you think it will sell quickly?'

'I can't say, love. With things the way they are just now, nobody could predict that, though it is a lovely place and you're asking a fair price. Anyhow,' he shrugged, getting to his feet, 'I have to go out now. I'm showing people over those offices we took on last month. Fingers crossed.'

'Just a minute——' Elaine felt a sudden rush of anxiety. The two other men involved in the business were out as well—Don's leaving the premises meant that she would be holding the fort. 'When will you be back? I mean—I mean, you know.' If anyone happened to want to view *Rosalie*, she did not want to be the one to accompany them. She had told Don this.

'No. What's wrong?' He shook his head at her. 'I see. You're worrying again! Will you try to be a little less uptight? You are not the inefficient twerp you seem to think yourself. You can cope. Besides, Pamela's here. There's nothing going on that she doesn't know about. She's a good girl, that.'

And Don was broad Lancashire. Elaine couldn't help smiling at his choice of words. A good girl, that! 'I know. It's just—what if someone enquires about *Rosalie*?'

'Elaine, it's only been on the market five minutes, don't expect miracles! In any case, Peter will be back by three, so you won't be left alone for long. 'Bye.'

Elaine took his advice when he'd gone. She sat back against the soft leather swivel chair, closed her eyes and made a conscious effort to relax. She was uptight, nervous, and it was high time she got a hold on it. It was so unlike her—understandable, all things considered, but unlike her none the less. Until six months ago she had been carefree, optimistic and happy. Maybe happy-go-lucky. She had never known responsibility, her parents had always supported her in what she wanted to do, even if they considered it odd. They had bought her a car, had paid the rent on the cottage for her, had supported her financially until she got her little business established.

On the other hand she had never been irresponsible, either. She had worked hard as far as her education was concerned, had passed every exam she had ever taken, insisted her parents stop helping her as soon as she could afford to keep herself. And she had been a good daughter; her conscience was clear on that. She had loved them dearly and had shown it, visiting almost every weekend and always——

'Miss Faraday?' Pamela was in the office, looking worried. 'I did knock, but you——'

'That's okay. What's up? You look upset.'

Pamela pushed the door to, jerking a thumb over her shoulder. 'I've got a right one out there, awkward as anything. He's asking—demanding—to see the boss. He was enquiring about your house, not that I mentioned it was your house, of course.'

Elaine looked at her blankly. 'Well, give him the details.'

'I have. He read through them and told me he wants to see the place today. Looks as if he hasn't got two ha'pennies to rub together, though I suppose you can never tell. Anyway, he's insisting on seeing *Rosalie* today.'

'But that's no problem. Ask him to come back at three o'clock, tell him Peter Tomkins will show him the property.'

'I can't.' Pamela sighed. 'Peter just phoned to say his car's broken down. He's stranded.'

'Oh. Er—what time is Keith due back?'

'It's Friday, Miss Faraday. Rent night.'

'Oh, yes.' Elaine put a hand to her temple. A headache had been threatening since lunchtime, a dull throbbing making itself felt now. It was hard to think. Friday was rent night, of course. Keith Shelley would be collecting rents until six or seven because Friday was also wages day—for those tenants who were in work. In the terraced properties her father had owned, rent had to be collected early Friday evening or else it might not get paid at all. In the area where the houses were, Friday night was very much beer-with-the-boys night.

How often had her father threatened to get rid of those properties? Maybe he'd been unable to. Still, they were under a Compulsory Purchase Order now; they wouldn't be a nuisance for much longer. Elaine would get the money for them, whatever that amounted to, and the problems of non-paying tenants would no longer be hers. God knew she had enough problems as things stood. 'Then ask this man to call in tomorrow morning. Tell him we open till noon on Saturday. If he wants——'

'I already have.' Pamela glanced over her shoulder at the closed door. 'He said he's going away for the weekend. Will you have a word with him? Honestly, he's really stroppy!' It was only when she added, 'Please?'

that Elaine agreed. She had never seen Pamela ruffled before.

'All right—but hang on a tick. Could you take him? I mean, if he's insisting, would you take him and show him *Rosalie*?'

The receptionist looked at her oddly. 'But I don't drive.'

'Maybe he's got a car——'

'It's possible he's got a push bike.' There was a grin. 'I can't go, Miss Faraday. Who'd look after the switchboard?'

As if on cue the phone started ringing in reception. Elaine hadn't the first clue about handling the switchboard. 'Send him in,' she said hastily. 'I'll sort something out.' She had no idea what she would sort out, and the throbbing at her temples wasn't helping any.

Pamela retreated gratefully, leaving the door open. Two seconds later Elaine's prospective buyer came in to her office. He was so tall that the top of his head was just inches short of the door frame. Six two? Six three? And Pamela was right, he looked like a pauper, was dressed in pale blue denim, jeans and shirt which were not merely washed-out but worn out. On his feet were a pair of battered leather sandals . . . and no socks.

Nevertheless Elaine moved swiftly around the desk to greet him, her hand outstretched. She did not judge people by the clothes they wore. Besides, there was a certain quality about the man, a presence which filled the room and had nothing to do with his size. His hair was magnificent, a riot of thick black curls which had her staring in admiration for a moment. Beneath heavy, jet black brows his eyes swept swiftly around the office, seemingly taking in every detail. They were striking eyes, grey and cold and hard. When they came to rest on Elaine they seemed to look right through her. She had the impression that he was not really seeing her, yet missing no detail.

Her smile was a little uncertain. 'Good afternoon, I'm——'

'I asked to see the boss,' he cut in rudely. 'What the hell does one have to do to get some service around here?' Elaine's mouth opened in surprise, his glare unnerving her. 'I'm sorry if . . . I am the boss, Mr . . .?'

'You?' His eyes raked over her openly now. 'You're telling me that you're in charge?'

She let her hand drop. 'I'm Elaine Faraday. I own the business.' She took a step backwards, puzzling about him. Pamela hadn't mentioned he was American. His accent was unmistakable, although she couldn't tell which part of the States he was from.

In the momentary silence, his eyes locked on to hers. He gave a curt nod, grunted and sat down before being invited to. 'Harris,' he said, 'the name's Harris. Guy Harris.'

Guy Harris . . . why did it ring a bell? She didn't know him from Adam. In his hand were the papers giving details about *Rosalie*. He waved them at her. 'This house is precisely what I'm looking for. Now, perhaps you can answer a question for me: would the owners be interested in letting the place? I'm only going to be around for six, maybe nine months.

'I'm afraid not. I—the owner wants to sell.' She immediately put him down as a time-waster, feeling no disappointment at all. She would be glad to be rid of him. The man made her nervous. His very assertiveness made her feel inadequate.

'No matter. Assuming the interior lives up to its description, I'll buy it, I can always sell when I'm ready to. And I'm talking cash.' He paused, letting his last words take effect. 'Call the owners and tell them we're on our way.'

Again her mouth opened, this time in astonishment. 'But——'

'But what?' Suddenly he was on his feet, dwarfing her as he leaned on the desk, looking straight into green eyes which reflected her confusion quite openly. 'What's the matter with you people? Either the house is for sale or it isn't. First the girl out there tells me there's no one available to show me around, then she tells me the owners aren't at home—without calling to check. Now you're looking at me as if I'm some kind of weirdo. What gives?'

'I'm—Mr Harris, I'm sorry. If you'll just bear with me a moment, I'll explain. The owner is—is away at the moment.'

'Then surely you have a key?'

'I—well, yes.' Elaine groaned inwardly. It would be much simpler to tell him she owned the property, but— but she didn't want to, for two reasons. It would be easier for someone else to negotiate a price with him. If he really had that much cash, he had bargaining power. She didn't want to be the one to show him *Rosalie*; she was too emotionally involved. Maybe it didn't make sense, but it was how she felt. There was something else, too, which again didn't make sense. She had only been in this man's company for two minutes, but she disliked him, didn't want him to be the one to buy her parents' home.

He was looking at her now with the air of one who was exercising a great deal of patience. 'Well, what are we waiting for?'

'Nothing.' The word came out dully. What choice did she have, really? He was a prospective buyer, a cash buyer at that. Given the state of the market just now, to refuse him would be madness. Wasn't she trying to sort out her life, at last? To get back to her own home and way of living? She *had* to be detached about all this, to let logic rule instead of emotion. What difference would it make to her who lived in *Rosalie*? Once it was sold, it was sold.

'Miss Faraday...' His deep voice cut into her thoughts, bringing her eyes back to his. 'I don't know whether lethargy is endemic in the north of England, I might simply have had bad luck so far in my dealings up here. Time will tell. You, however, are the sleepiest specimen I've encountered to date. How you stay in business, I cannot imagine. I've been in Lancashire all week, scouring the area for a suitable house. I appear to have found one. *If* I can get a look at it. I'm leaving for the south very early in the morning, so do you think—if it's not too much trouble, and I am loath to interrupt your daydreaming—that we could see this property today?'

Elaine experienced a strong ripple of anger. Nothing had moved her to anger for a long time, for years in fact, but this man had managed it. God, what sarcasm! She looked away, picking up her handbag as she got to her feet. 'Mr Harris, I shall take you, personally, to view the house. Right now.'

'You don't say!'

She clamped her lips together. He beat her to the door, opening it with an exaggerated bow as he let her precede him. She cleared her throat. 'My car's on the——'

'We'll use mine. It's right outside the door.'

'On double yellow lines? Did you realise——'

He interrupted yet again. 'If I've been given a ticket, I know you'll be only too pleased to pay the fine. Take it out of your commission. After all, I'll have you to thank for it.'

She didn't look at him. She looked at Pamela, who was busy typing. 'Pam, I'll be out for an hour or so. I'm taking Mr Harris to view *Rosalie*.'

Pamela nodded and smiled diplomatically.

There were in fact two cars parked illegally outside, a Mini and a Porsche. Neither of the two extremes suited

Guy Harris' image. He was far too tall for a Mini and——

His was the Porsche. It was very handsome, sleek and silver. Already he was opening the door to the passenger seat. Elaine got in, her bewilderment and curiosity increasing by the minute. A *Porsche*, for heaven's sake! She looked at the luxurious interior and then at the driver. Who was he? What was he? And why should a rich American want to live in the industrial north of England? He wasn't a business man, surely? The way he was dressed was . . . maybe he was in the music business?

Without realising it, she was staring at him now. Guy Harris, Guy Harris. Was he a singer? A pop singer? No, he was a little old for that. Middle thirties, probably.

'You're doing it again, Miss Faraday.' He sighed heavily, his cold grey eyes rolling heavenward. 'I'm waiting for you to direct me.'

She directed him. Apart from that she said nothing at all as he drove quickly but with a crisp efficiency which she had gathered was part of his nature. This man knew what he wanted and went after it, he liked action, results. Yet he looked like—like an off-duty fisherman or something. A handsome one, she had to admit. Her eyes slid to his hands, though she had already noticed them in the office. Nails and teeth were the first things she noticed about people. In his case both were clean and strong, white, well looked after.

It was only as they were approaching the house that she ventured a question. 'Are you a family man, Mr Harris?'

'Sort of.'

That ought to have stopped her. It certainly irritated but it also intrigued her further. 'I meant—well, this house has three bedrooms. Four if the study were——'

'Uh-huh.'

She felt it again, that ripple of anger. But it still didn't

stop her. 'You're working in the north then, are you?'
'Not yet.'

That was enough. She shrugged. 'I'm sorry, I should mind my own business.'

'Yes. Why don't you do that?'

To her horror, tears sprang into her eyes. She turned away at once, feeling foolish and absurdly conscious of his disapproval. She was also conscious of his proximity. He was a big man, not only very tall but also broad and solidly built. He was all muscle. For just an instant her imagination ran amok. Wasn't she in a vulnerable position, come to think of it? Getting into a car with a total stranger, about to show him around her home, alone. He was a nasty piece of work.

Elaine bit hard into her cheeks in an effort to compose herself, distract herself with self-inflicted pain. How very stupid she was being. Her increasing nervous tension was affecting her to a ridiculous extent. Curt and downright rude he might be, but it didn't mean he was a potential rapist. She shouldn't feel so intimidated, nor should she have asked personal questions. She shook her head as if to clear it—her headache was of the fuzzy kind. She felt as though it were full of cotton wool. 'That's the entrance to the drive, about two hundred yards ahead on the left,' she told him.

Guy Harris swung the car on to the gravel drive leading to the house, which stood well back from the road. He brought it to a halt right outside the front door and was out of the car before she had a chance to say anything else. Again he opened the car door for her. This was something else which didn't fit; this courtesy did not go with his curtness.

On the ground floor of the house they walked from room to room, Elaine answering his questions. There weren't many. Everything was spick and span in the comfortable home with which she was so familiar, it had been redecorated throughout less than a year ago. From the kitchen she led the way in to the double garage so he could see just how spacious it was.

Upstairs, once they reached the second bathroom, she opened the cabinet on the wall and took two aspirin from a bottle. Her bedroom came next, then the guest room and finally her parents' bedroom with its en suite bathroom.

'Fine. It's fine.' Guy Harris stood facing her, frowning slightly. Again his eyes were penetrating, giving the impression now of looking right inside her head. When next he spoke, she detected a change in him. 'Do you think the owners would be outraged if we made ourselves a cup of coffee while we talk business?'

His searching look and the sudden softness of his voice almost threw her. 'No, I—I'm sure they wouldn't. Let's—go downstairs.'

Mr Harris waited in the living room while she made the coffee. She found him looking totally at home sitting on one of the two settees which faced one another either side of the fireplace. Her mother had insisted on having a gas fire in this room despite the central heating. She liked—had liked—a focal point and the fire was one of those marvellous imitation coal efforts which had flames, looking as real as any real one.

Elaine carefully placed the tray on a side table, asked how he liked his coffee and handed him a cup. She settled herself on the opposite settee.

'I like the house,' she was informed. 'It's just what I—er—need. Yes, need is the right word. Moreover I like the furnishings and decorations. There's nothing to do, it's ready to walk in to. I'd like to buy the lot, Miss Faraday, everything included—and I mean everything, right down to the last teaspoon.'

She was gaping at him again.

'Please stop doing that. You might have a headache

but you're not deaf. Well, what do you say?'

'I—I'll have to enquire . . .' It was all getting out of hand, all a bit much. He wanted to buy *everything*? It was too good to be true, really. From her point of view it would be so very convenient . . . yet an incredible sadness was enveloping her, bringing with it the threat of tears she knew she would not be able to check this time.

'Miss Faraday?' Now it was the extreme gentleness of his voice that startled her. He was still watching her, had not taken his eyes off her. She had felt his gaze even as she'd been staring down at the carpet. 'Why don't you spill it out? What *is* going on with you? This is your house, isn't it? Or, at least, it belongs to relatives. You know every inch of the place, not to mention knowing where the aspirin are kept. Apart from that there was a photo by the bed in the second bedroom. A man and a woman, a woman whose eyes are identical to yours. Your mother?'

Elaine didn't even know there were tears sliding down her cheeks. They were just coming of their own accord, silently, softly. 'My mother,' she confirmed. 'It—it was my mother.'

And then, quite suddenly, she was sobbing. Guy Harris was by her side in a flash, taking both her hands in his. Elaine snatched them away, recoiling from him. She was appalled at herself, acutely embarrassed at her outburst. All this was manifested as anger—anger at herself and resurrected anger at him. 'Don't do that! Get away from me. Get out of my house! I don't like your attitude, I don't like you, and you're the last person in the world I'd sell *Rosalie* to!'

He stayed where he was. He wasn't touching her, wasn't moving a muscle. He was staring at her. 'Good God . . . what did I say?'

Elaine was scrabbling in her bag for a hanky. Wordlessly, he handed her one, snow-white and beautifully pressed. She took it because she had no choice, she was snuffling and streaming, feeling like the biggest idiot on earth. She simply couldn't stop crying, couldn't get control of herself.

The man by her side waited patiently, silently, but her tears kept coming. After several minutes his arms went around her shoulders. There was only a momentary resistance as he pulled her firmly against his massive chest. 'Take it easy now. Come on, whatever it is, it's not the end of the world. You may think it is right now, but it isn't.'

Elaine wasn't thinking at all. A fresh bout of sobbing racked her body and she leaned limply against him, not even realising what she was saying. It just came out in a garbled stream. 'She's d-dead. They're both dead. They were killed! It—this was their house and if I sell it, it will be as if they never existed, in a way. I know that's not true, it's silly to feel ... But it's like wiping out twenty years, you see. I—Dad had this house built when I was two ... I lived ... I lived ...'

'It's all right,' he was saying softly. 'I understand. Believe it or not, I understand precisely how you're feeling.'

It was the odd note in his voice that brought her to her senses. She wriggled out of his grasp, blowing her nose noisily and glancing at him from beneath lowered lashes. 'It's kind of you to say that.' She managed a smile. 'I don't believe you for an instant, but it's kind of you to say it. I—Mr Harris, I'll have to think——'

'Guy,' he said firmly. 'Make it Guy, will you?' He got to his feet. 'You okay now?'

She nodded, still embarrassed.

'Right, here's what we'll do. I'll drive you back to your office. You will think over what I've proposed. Make a list of the house's contents and their value; I'm not going to haggle over a few dollars here or there. If you're prepared to sell everything to me—apart from the things you want to keep, of course—it'll save me the headache of buying things, making the place habitable. A time saving.' He nodded as if satisfied. 'So far so good. I'll come back tonight, here, at around seven. I'm sorry to rush you like this, but I have a lot to organise. We'll talk then. Over dinner.'

'Dinner? Oh, I don't think——'

'*Over dinner.* On neutral ground. Perhaps then you will be able to think—more clearly.'

Elaine was in a daze when she got back to the office. She sat at the big oak desk thinking not about the man's offer but the man himself. He had thrown her in to a spin several times what with his initial aggression, his forcefulness, his proposition and then—then the kindness, the memory of which was holding her in a state of bemusement now. It was as if she had met two different people rolled into one. The net result was that she still felt silly, though he clearly hadn't thought that of her, and the prospect of facing him again was not a welcome one.

But it was business. By selling not only the house but also its contents, she would be saving him a lot of inconvenience, he had said. That was certainly the case with her. It was the most civilised way of disposing of her parents' furniture that she could think of. She hadn't cherished the idea of selling it off in bits and pieces or letting a 'house clearance' merchant come along and insult her with a poor offer.

When Don got back to the office at a little after four, Elaine discussed the matter with him. He was staggered at what he saw as her 'amazing luck'.

'It's incredible, Elaine. That photograph must have been in our window less than half an hour. In he walks, offers you the asking price, ready cash, and takes all the contents, too! You want my opinion? Snatch his hand off!'

Don was right, of course, yet she couldn't help feeling a stab of resentment towards him. Didn't he realise how painful this was for her?

'Mind you,' he went on, 'nothing's final till you see the colour of his money. What does he do for a living?'

'I've no idea.'

'You're absolutely certain he was serious?'

'Yes. He was driving a Porsche, if that tells you anything.'

'Not necessarily. It doesn't mean he's genuine.' He got up. 'Well, I'll leave you to make your list. Would you like me to be there when he calls to see you tonight?'

Elaine avoided his eyes. She had told Don about her appointment with her buyer but not that he was taking her out to dinner. Now why had she omitted to mention that? 'No, I—I can cope, thanks.'

She didn't mention it to Pamela, either, when she came in a few minutes later. She told her everything but.

'Oh, Miss Faraday, that's marvellous! I mean—I mean, well, it'll save you a few problems, won't it? Selling the furniture and that.'

'I suppose so. Yes, it will.'

'Isn't it odd? I took an instant dislike to that man.'

'So did I.'

'He was gorgeous, though, wasn't he? Rude, but handsome!'

'I can't say I noticed, Pamela . . . Any chance of a cup of tea?'

By six-thirty that evening Elaine had a bad case of the jitters. Guy Harris had crowded her mind all afternoon. All she wanted now was to get things over with. The list was ready, her asking prices written at the side of each item. She would go over it with him, make sure he agreed that what she was asking was fair, given the age and condition of the various things. The carpets and curtains were included in the asking price in any case, as were the light fittings.

She had changed her clothes but she had just changed her mind, too; there really was no reason to go out to dinner with him. It would be too pathetic of her not to be able to conduct the business herself right here. She had been so much better lately, so much less emotional. Quite what had happened to her this afternoon, she wasn't sure. Guy Harris had been partly responsible. He had made her nervous. She was still tense. The sooner everything was handed over to solicitors, the better. About half an hour with him tonight would be enough, then he would be out of her life as quickly as he'd crashed in to it.

When it got to ten past seven, she thought he wasn't going to turn up. She was wrong.

When she opened the door to him, her breath caught in her throat. 'Mr Harris ... good heavens!'

Impressions, so many impressions were coming at her. Guy Harris was standing on her doorstep with a bouquet of white roses wrapped in cellophane, tied with an enormous bow. Her glance moved from the flowers to his eyes and then to his hair, which shocked her all over again in its intensely black magnificence. There was so much of it, so thick and curly ... But it was his clothes which had brought the exclamation to her lips. He was dressed in a beige, lightweight suit with contrasting shirt and tie. It fitted to perfection, was cut immaculately.

'Guy.' And he was smiling. It changed everything about him. 'Well? Have I to stand on your doorstep all evening or are we going to have a drink before we go out?'

'I——' Elaine felt gauche, positively gauche. He looked so—so *sophisticated*. 'Please come in.'

She took the flowers from him in the living room, blushing her thanks. He seemed amused. It didn't help. 'Please—sit down. I'll get a vase and pour you a drink.'

'I'd rather have it in a glass, if it's all the same to you.'
She turned, her eyes widening. 'Oh! I meant——'

'I know what you meant.' He walked over to her and put both hands on her shoulders. 'Elaine, will you please try to relax? Those flowers are my way of apologising. I was extremely unpleasant this afternoon and I can only plead mitigating circumstances. I've had a very frustrating week, one of those where everything goes wrong, you know the sort. And on my way in to Bury today, I had a blow-out on the motorway. Just as I thought my luck had changed, I had your receptionist to contend with. I thought there was something odd in the way she talked to me about this house, but I had no idea——'

'It wasn't her fault. I'd given instructions—well, it doesn't matter now, does it?'

'Not in the least. May I sit down?'

'Please do.' She went into the kitchen, her mind racing yet again. What a contrast to the man she'd met only a few hours earlier! His clothes . . . and what about his attitude? Was he on his best behaviour or something, because he wanted to make a deal with her? Or was this what he was really like? *What* was he? And what had he meant when he'd told her he was 'sort of' a family man?

It wasn't something she normally drank, but she joined him when he asked for a whisky with soda. Her father's bar, built into a recess, was well stocked. She got down to business then, taking the list from her handbag.

'I've listed everything,' she began, but he held up a hand in warning. 'Not now, Elaine.'

'But——'

'Later. We have the entire evening.'

'Ah! As a matter of fact, we haven't. You see, I'd planned on going home this evening——'

'Home? You don't actually live here then?'

'No. Just temporarily until—until I've got everything sorted out. Anyway, about dinner, I appreciate your offer but it really isn't necessary to take me out.'

'Necessary? God, you're so formal! Even more than the average Englishwoman. Of course it isn't *necessary*. But it might be fun, and it's my guess that you're long overdue for a little fun, Miss Elaine Faraday.'

Elaine was stuck for words. She became suspicious again. What did he have in mind, exactly? With extreme politeness she said, 'I really don't think that's any of your business.'

He inclined his head. 'All right, I'll respect that. But you're coming out with me, I won't take no for an answer. That's something which doesn't come easily to me.'

She had gathered that. She sighed. 'All right, Mr Harris, so be it.'

'*Guy*!'

Again she sighed. 'Guy.'

Had she known where he was taking her for dinner she would have worn something more dressy than the cotton shift she had put on, not that she had much that was appropriate to choose from. The Hotel Piccadilly in the centre of Manchester was probably the best in town, but it was not her scene. Sophistication and ultra-smart surroundings were not familiar to Elaine. Her parents had remarked often that she was more a country girl than a city girl. They hadn't known why this proved to be so; neither did she, come to that. But she was more at home in the country; she liked mucking about in clothes which were comfortable, gardening, and working at her craft. Her idea of a good evening out, not that she went out much, was one spent with friends, in a country pub, or her home or theirs, enjoying good, basic dinners which didn't cost the earth. She had several friends—girls she'd been to school with, most of whom were married but as yet childless.

She did, however, know how to conduct herself wherever she was. Her parents had always stayed in smart hotels when they had taken her on holidays. They were . . . she quelled the thought. Holidays. They'd been going on holiday when their plane had crashed. Determinedly she plunged into conversation with her host. 'Are you staying here?'

'At this hotel?' It was as if she'd asked a silly question. 'No.'

'I just wondered why you'd brought me here.'

'I thought it would please you, thought it would be your sort of place. I was told this is one of the best hotels in town.'

Elaine smiled inwardly, amused by the impression he had formed of her. He was way off beam! 'Where are you staying, then?' she asked.

'At an inn, out in the country. Bang on the border of Lancashire and Yorkshire.'

'Your wife prefers a quiet place, does she?' No sooner were the words out than she regretted them. God, how obvious he would think her! He would misunderstand that question, for sure. She was not trying to establish whether he were married, she was just generally curious about him. Very.

The curtness was back. 'I don't have a wife.'

That's *it*, she vowed. No more personal questions, I swear it. She picked up the menu, chatting as she did so, determined not to allow tension to come between them again. It would be so much nicer if their business could be conducted without more unpleasantness. This man was a closed book when it came to——

She almost dropped the menu. She had just realised who he was! Guy Harris was a writer, a very well-known writer. No wonder the name had rung a bell, it was hardly surprising! If she had read anything by him, she would have recognised the name at once, of course. But she hadn't read any of his work. Reading was one of her pastimes, but she had always assumed his books were not her cup of tea. She had given them a cursory glance when she'd been in bookshops but that was all. He didn't write modern-day fiction, which she preferred. Don Black sprang into her mind and she had to suppress a giggle. Wait till he heard about this! He had wondered whether her prospective buyer was genuine.

He was genuine all right. Elaine knew nothing about Guy Harris the writer except that he was American. Which was as much as she knew about Guy Harris the man. She should have put two and two together before now. Hadn't she actually glanced at his photo on the jackets of his books?

The temptation to tell him she had realised who he was, to bombard him with questions, was overwhelming. She resisted it. There was no way she wanted to get her head bitten off again. Still, she couldn't resist looking at him. He was reading the menu, unaware of her scrutiny as she took in the details of his face with renewed interest. A lean face with a firm, determined jaw, straight nose and well-shaped mouth. The light was casting a shadow on his cheeks from his downturned lashes, as black as his heavy brows, and Elaine was smiling slightly at this when he suddenly looked at her.

'And so?' Fortunately he was grinning.

And fortunately she was unruffled. 'Am I allowed a personal remark?'

'What can I say to that? I'm intrigued.'

'You're a man of contrasts, Mr—Guy. Earlier in the day I'd have sworn you had as much sensitivity as the bumpers on your car.'

'So what's changed your mind?'

She couldn't tell him. His kindness when she had cried, for one thing. The fact that he was a writer, for another. Creative people were not insensitive, not in her experience, even if they managed to give the impression that they were. Instead she smiled warmly and resorted to the mundane, side-stepping his question. 'You look so smart tonight. This afternoon I could have been forgiven for thinking you a tramp.'

'If you keep smiling at me like that, I'll forgive you anything!'

She laughed. 'Don't bother flirting with me, if that's what you're doing, because it will get you precisely nowhere.'

'Oh, don't worry on that score, all I'm after is your property.' He said it lightly, flippantly, but the message came over loud and clear: you're not my type. Her reaction to it was curious, she didn't know whether to be relieved or disappointed.

Throughout dinner their conversation was kept strictly to things general, but it flowed easily and without any strain at all. The wine must have helped. Whatever, Elaine did relax. She felt more relaxed than she had since the death of her parents all those months ago. It was over coffee that they got down to business. Guy didn't argue, didn't question her prices at all. He made it so easy! 'There are a few things not listed, things which have sentimental value, which I'll be taking to my own home.'

'Naturally.'

She looked at him, intensely serious. 'Why are you so accepting, why aren't you arguing, bartering? You even accepted the asking price on the property without a protest.'

'It isn't a fair price?'

'Certainly, but one always——'

'One always—what? Time is money, but in this particular instance time is more valuable to me than money. I want to settle in *Rosalie* as soon as possible. Obviously I have my reasons.'

'Obviously.'

He, too, was intensely serious now. 'Do we have a deal, Elaine?'

'Yes indeed.' She held out her hand across the table. He shook it. The contact startled her, his grasp was warm and firm and—oddly disturbing. 'Shall we go?' she asked crisply.

'Must we? I'm enjoying myself . . . more than I have in a long time, actually.'

'You—you said you had to make an early start in the morning.'

'That doesn't matter. I never have trouble waking up. On the contrary.'

It was the first tit-bit of information he had volunteered about himself and Elaine found herself filing it away as if it were important.

It was turned eleven when he pulled up outside *Rosalie*. 'I'll see you safely inside.'

She didn't argue. It wasn't her safety she was worried about, it was the very emptiness of this house that bothered her, every single time she walked in to it, something which never affected her in her own home. It was for this reason that she asked Guy if he would like a nightcap or a cup of coffee. At least, she told herself it was.

'Better make it coffee since I'm driving. Thank you.'

Pleased because he seemed pleased, Elaine went in to the kitchen to put the kettle on. She emerged to find him looking at a photograph of her parents, a wedding photo which stood on top of the bookcase. It looked very dated now, but it was a favourite of hers.

'It would have been their silver wedding anniversary next month,' she told him.

He looked at her, gauging her mood. 'What happened to them, Elaine?'

She told him, her voice steady, in no danger of breaking down again. 'They were on that Seven-four-seven which crashed last January.'

'The one that took off from Heathrow? Oh, my God . . .'

Elaine looked down at her hands. The plane had crashed shortly after take-off. There had been some survivors but . . . 'They were going away to the sun for a couple of weeks. They always went away in January because it's a quiet time in the business. They'd been staying with my aunt and uncle at their house in London, they were all going away together. My aunt, my uncle and their two elder sons, both of whom were with their wives. One of them was four months pregnant. They all died, Guy, the entire family—families. I'm left with one cousin, my uncle's younger son who's just finished at Oxford University.'

Guy put the photograph down, saying nothing. What could he say? What could anyone say in the face of such tragedy? In relief, tactfully, he changed the subject. 'I think the kettle's just boiled. Let me make the coffee, might as well start finding where things are.'

He came back two minutes later with a tray, during which time Elaine had powdered her nose and flicked a comb through her hair.

'I'll tell you what clinched your sale to me today,' he said, 'it was the fact that the house is detached, has a bit of space around it, isn't overlooked. I hope the neighbours aren't the nosy, intrusive kind.'

She accepted a cup of coffee from him, smiling. 'I think that'll be up to you. They're pleasant people, but they won't come calling if you don't encourage it.'

'I won't. I need my privacy. Mine is a very solitary profession, I'm a writer.'

Her smile widened. 'I know. I realised earlier who you are.'

Guy's eyebrows went up. 'And you said nothing?'

'Like what? I can't tell you I'm one of your biggest fans, I haven't read any of your work.'

He laughed at that, really laughed. His head went back and he roared with it, keeping Elaine's eyes riveted on him in fascination. He looked so—so different, so much younger when all that intensity was chased from his face. 'How blunt! And how very refreshing! Normally I get assailed with questions, always the same questions, which is why I don't readily volunteer what I do.'

'Yet you use your own name. If you really want to protect your privacy, why not use a pen-name?'

'Because in the early days—well, I didn't think about that till it was too late. I didn't realise how successful my first book would be. Once the name Guy Harris was established, I could hardly change it.'

Elaine hesitated, unsure whether she dared ask what she was so curious to find out. 'At the risk of being predictable, may I ask you a question?'

'Fire away.'

'Why the devil do you want to live in Tottington for six or nine months?'

It clearly wasn't what he had been expecting. 'Because of its geography. Bury is just down the road. From here I can be in the centre of Manchester in forty minutes or so, with access to its extremely good library. I can cover the whole of Lancashire and Yorkshire in a day and——' He broke off, smiling at her. 'Perhaps I should have started by telling you my next book is set in this area. Around the beginning of the century. One of the major characters is a mill-owner, one of "England's dark, satanic".'

'The mill or the man?'

'Both. Anyhow, I have a lot of research to do, and I like to be on the spot when I'm writing about a place, actually living there. It adds verisimilitude.'

'Even though you're here about eighty years too late?'

'The research will take care of that.'

But still she persisted. 'Why *buy* a house? It seems a bit extreme.'

'It is. But I couldn't find a suitable one to rent.'

'Then why not work from a hotel, this inn you're staying at?'

He grinned. 'Are you trying to talk yourself out of a sale or something?'

'No, I'm just curious.'

'Well, it's quite simple. I work odd hours, when the mood takes me. Sometimes I go on through the night. There's that, and the clatter of the word processor I use—or rather the printer. I need complete freedom without interruptions. I also like my creature comforts. It's infinitely preferable to be in my own place.' He paused, smiling. 'And now it's your turn.' When she looked at him blankly, he elaborated. 'To tell me something about yourself.'

Elaine put her coffee cup back on the tray. 'I'm not half as interesting,' she said dismissively. He didn't really want to know about her—why should he? He was only being polite.

'I see. You're about to throw me out, is that it?'

So she'd been right. She knew a sense of disappointment again, but hid it well. 'Exactly!' she laughed. 'But I must thank you for a very pleasant evening. You were right, it was fun.'

They had almost reached the door when he asked her about solicitors. 'I don't know anyone in the area, Elaine. Can you recommend someone?'

'No problem. We're well in with several.'

'I want completion as quickly as possible. It would speed things up if we both used the same firm—but I'm not sure whether they'll wear that.'

'I doubt it.' She stepped back into the living room and wrote down a name and telephone number. 'Here you are. Mr Prentis is excellent, ask him to be as quick as he can as a special favour to me. I'll instruct my solicitor likewise. There'll be no problem, no delays, don't worry.'

He smiled at her last two words. She had no idea why. 'Well, goodnight, Guy.'

He was still smiling, looking down at her from his superior height. For an instant she had the stupid notion that he was going to kiss her. Worse, she actually found herself hoping he would.

But he didn't. He merely inclined his head and bade her goodnight.

At one o'clock in the morning Elaine was still thinking about Guy, about the evening, about the events of the day from the moment she'd met him. Her mind was teeming with it, all of it. Mainly she was trying to work out why she felt . . . well, if not exactly light-hearted, she certainly felt as though a weight had been lifted from her shoulders. Selling *Rosalie* was sad, yet she could not deny her feeling of relief at having solved a problem, several problems, since Guy Harris was buying the contents, too. There was also satisfaction in actually having made a decision, in having acted positively at last, which was something she had been unable to do recently.

At two o'clock she was still awake, still thinking, still feeling pleased with herself. The manner in which she had told Guy about her family's death had been something of a milestone, too. For the first time ever she had spoken of it without crying, with a measure of acceptance which had enabled her to remain calm.

Quite apart from all that, she had enjoyed this evening. It was almost comical, recalling how nervous, how jittery she had been at the prospect of having dinner with Guy. It had all been so easy, really! There was no denying he'd been right in telling her she was long overdue for some fun. She hadn't smiled so much for what seemed like ages. He had even managed to make her laugh a few times.

At a quarter to three Elaine was still awake—but by then she was angry with herself. Thoughts of Guy, of the man himself, were keeping her awake now. Why did he intrigue her so? Why had she known a certain relief in hearing he didn't have a wife? It was too ridiculous. If Guy himself had anything to do with her change of mood, she wasn't going to admit it.

At a quarter past three she reached into the bedside drawer for what remained of the sleeping tablets she had been given months ago by her doctor. There were half a dozen left in the bottle, but that had been the—what?— fourth or fifth bottle. She had stopped taking them only five weeks ago. It was that thought which prevented her from taking some now. In fact she was appalled for having considered it; she was damned if she would take sleeping pills just because there was a man on her mind!

She turned over and thumped her pillow, resenting Guy Harris' intrusion. What on earth was the matter with her? Why, when she closed her eyes, did she keep seeing his face in detail so clear, so sharp that he might have been in the bed with her?

CHAPTER TWO

THE gardens around Elaine's cottage seemed to have run amok. It had been only a week since she had last come home—a week of sunshine which had done wonders for the weeds as well as everything else. She got out of her car in the middle of the morning, regretting her shortage of sleep—she should have got here earlier. Damn Guy Harris. He was still in her thoughts. She circled her home slowly, mentally calculating how long it would take to get her gardens back in order as she liked them.

When she finally opened her front door, however, all thoughts of gardening and of Guy were instantly pushed aside. There was a stack of post on the doormat. Most of it was orders, special orders.

Elaine pored over it while drinking a cup of coffee. It was most unusual to get so many special orders within the space of a week. The shops she sold to, gift shops mostly, catered to visitors and tourists; they normally took whatever she had to offer. But there they were—seven special orders for delivery as soon as possible. She was pleased but she was also a little panicky: she had hoped to spend time replenishing her stock this weekend. It was the middle of the summer, and the items she had created during the winter had almost all been sold.

She sat a while longer, thinking, planning the coming week. Her mind made up, she telephoned Don Black at the office. 'Don? Hello, I'm glad I caught you before you left——'

His chuckle interrupted her. 'You can always ring me at home, you know!'

'Yes, but—never mind. Listen, Don, I won't be

coming in to the office next week. I got home to find a stack of orders waiting for me. Well, seven!' she smiled. For her, seven constituted a stack.

If she had expected Don to be pleased for her, she was mistaken. 'That's your prerogative, of course. But— Elaine, we do need another pair of hands around here. Have you—well, have you thought about my offer? About the business? When can I expect a decision?'

The business. She groaned inwardly. She had to make another decision. 'Don, I'm sorry but I'm still a bit vague about your proposal. I'll have to ask you to go over it again.'

'It's all right.' There was a smile in his voice; he really was a nice man. 'As a matter of fact, things have changed a little. I've had another idea or two, I can make you a better offer now. I can't explain it over the phone. I know you're busy, but if you could spare me an hour——'

'Of course I can. I'll see you tomorrow if you like.'

'Great! Let's have lunch. I'll come and pick you up.'

'No, that's okay. I'll meet you half-way.' She was thinking of a suitable meeting place, but Don beat her to it. He suggested a pub about half-way between her home and Bury and they arranged to meet at noon.

Elaine put the phone down slowly, thoughtful. No commitment. All she had promised Don was that she would listen to his proposals. She would listen carefully this time and then she would have to decide what to do. It was only fair to him. In the meantime . . . 'Come on,' she told herself. 'Get moving. This isn't getting the baby washed!'

She worked solidly, and happily, for the rest of the day. In the early evening she went out to water the garden. Her eyes were tired and she wouldn't be able to work any longer—she could not be creative to order. If she spent the next week dividing her time between her work, the housework and the gardening, everything would get done. Her world would never be the same again, but, slowly, slowly, she was at least getting her life back in order.

That was her second thought on waking on Sunday morning. Her life, routine, yes, but what of herself? Guy Harris had been her first thought; he had been in her mind on waking. Had she dreamt about him? If so, she couldn't remember. She hoped not. Never yet had she met a man who trespassed so much on her mind. It really was a nuisance.

On Sunday evening she sat herself down and made a conscious effort to reach a decision about the proposals Don had put to her about taking over the business. She couldn't. She needed help, a professional opinion.

On Monday morning she phoned her solicitor, a long-standing friend of the family. He listened, grunting now and then, and gave her his opinion when she'd finished.

Elaine bit her lower lip, dissatisfied. Mr Jackson was not being very helpful. In the end he told her it had to be her decision. She knew that already! 'I see. Er—there's another matter, Mr Jackson. About the house . . .'

But he already knew about the sale of *Rosalie*. Mr Prentis had been in touch with him, which meant that Guy Harris had been in touch with Mr Prentis. Elaine found herself relieved at that. She still couldn't believe her luck. 'And you'll press on as fast as possible? When can we expect completion?'

In four or five weeks, was the answer. Well, that was satisfactory, at least. Four or five weeks was quick; solicitors were not renowned for galloping through the conveyancing procedures.

Again she was thoughtful on hanging up. Four or five weeks. It meant that by the middle of August *Rosalie* would be no more, as far as she was concerned. She would have to remove all the things she wanted to keep.

She might need to hire a van. Something else to think about.

'But not right now. Get to work, Elaine!' She was talking to herself again, she never used to. That was something which had not yet returned to normal and possibly never would. Oh, she was coming back to life, keeping her business ticking over—but it wasn't the same, even here, in the cottage. The contentment she had once known was . . . changed. It was and it was not there. She shook herself. Of course it wasn't. She had lost all but one member of her family, a cousin who lived two hundred miles away. Philip must be feeling the same way: alone, really alone in the world. Perhaps, when winter came and things were quiet again, she would go and stay with him for a week or two. He must be rattling around in that big house his parents had left, now he had finished his education.

The rain on Tuesday and Wednesday put paid to any gardening. Elaine was ensconced in her work-room for the best part of both days and spent the rest of her time doing much-neglected housework. On Thursday morning she drove to the nearest supermarket and stocked up her freezer, keeping aside a loin of chops she planned on roasting for dinner. She frowned as she got out of her car: two days of rain and the garden needed weeding again. Well, she could do it, the sunshine was back. She unpacked her shopping, changed into her oldest denims and the skimpiest tee-shirt she could find, and set about the garden on the south side of the cottage.

She was in the back garden when Guy Harris turned up. It was almost six o'clock, and had she not taken her transistor radio out with her, she would have heard the car approaching. As it was, the sound of the music drowned it out, and her first awareness of not being alone was the sudden feeling that she was being watched.

Very slowly she turned, in a kneeling position by the

flower beds, a ripple of alarm moving along her spine.
When her eyes came to rest on Guy leaning on a wall,
watching her, Elaine's heart flipped crazily and it was all
she could do to prevent herself from snapping at him. She
didn't want to feel so pleased to see him, didn't want him
to see her looking such a wreck.

'Guy! How did you—what are you doing here?' Self-
consciously she got to her feet, switching off the radio.
He was staring at her. No wonder. Her hands and her
bare feet were filthy, perspiration had the tee-shirt
clinging to her body, and her hair, which needed
washing, was in elastic bands in two bunches that made
her look about ten years old.

'Well, well, well,' he drawled as she approached him.
'What have we here? And you said *I* was a man of
contrasts. What about this for a change of image? You
look beautiful, Elaine, very beautiful.'

She gaped at him. Incredibly, he meant it. He wasn't
smiling, his grey eyes were intense, scanning her face,
moving slowly over the length of her body. 'Guy? Have
you gone mad?'

'Oh, I approve,' he told her. 'Back to nature. No make-
up, no perfume . . . and no bra.'

She spluttered in indignation. 'Do you *mind*! What—
how did you find me?'

'I looked around the back of the house, followed the
source of the music, and there you were.'

Elaine was flustered, very, he was still looking at her
intently and though it seemed unbelievable to her, his
compliment had been sincere. 'You know very well
what——' Before she could say anything else he caught
hold of her hair, holding the two bunches at right-angles
and laughing.

'I'm not sure about these,' he said, 'though I suppose
there's a certain cuteness——'

'Will you stop that?'—she slapped his hands away,

hardly knowing what to do with herself. Her heart was racing and she was blushing like a schoolgirl. What was the matter with her? She was so damned pleased to see him. 'Since you're here, you might as well come in. I—I must wash my hands.'

She trooped into the kitchen, acutely aware of his soft tread behind her. He looked different, too, he also was wearing a tee-shirt which showed every contour of his chest, solid and muscular and . . . Elaine stuck her hands under the tap, trying to compose herself, unwilling to look at him for the moment. She didn't need to. And very attractive, was the end of her thought. The washed-out denims were the ones he had been wearing when she met him but she didn't even notice their scruffiness today. The man made the clothes irrelevant. 'Well,' she said gaily, 'since you're here, can I offer you a beer or something? Guy?'

He had vanished. He had walked through to the living room, was looking around as though her modest little home were a mansion. 'So this is where you live! What a gorgeous place, I love it! How long have you been here, and how did you make such a find?' He gave her no chance to answer, his enthusiasm amusing her no end.

Gorgeous? Well, Elaine thought so, but she didn't expect a man such as Guy to be so appreciative. She had made the cottage cosy, putting her own stamp on it, expressing her personality. The walls were emulsioned in the very palest lemon so there was only a hint of the colour. It was added to on a sunny day like this, giving a soft glow to the room. Next to the fireplace was a chintz armchair and opposite that a two-seater settee. There wasn't enough room for a second chair, a bigger settee. A couple of occasional tables and lamps, a small writing desk by the window, and the room was full. The curtains and carpets were plain, natural-coloured, the walls dotted with paintings and ornamental plates, but what

pleased her most of all were her plants. Tucked in corners
and hanging in baskets from the ceiling were houseplants
of all shapes and sizes. In Elaine's opinion it was these
more than anything else that softened the room, made it
look cosy.

'From whom did you inherit green fingers?' was Guy's
next question. 'This is a first class specimen, eh?
Nephrolepis exaltata Bostoniensis, one of my favourite
houseplants.'

'My very favourite.' Elaine couldn't help laughing at
him. 'But I call it a Boston fern.'

'That's what I said.' He grinned, spotting the door at
the far side of the room and heading for it. 'What's
through here? May I look?'

She trailed after him. He hadn't waited for an answer.
It was only the bathroom.

'Bathroom downstairs. A bit eccentric but convenient,
I suppose. Upstairs?'

Elaine shrugged. 'Go right ahead.' He would anyway.
The staircase led off from the tiniest hall, behind the
front door. She let him go first, laughing openly now.
There were only two rooms upstairs, her bedroom and
the one she had converted into a work-room.

Guy explored the bedroom first, casting an eye over
the sloping roof with open rafters, the double bed and
built-in wardrobes, the white, shaggy rugs on the wooden
floor. He pronounced this room, 'Delightful,' before
turning to her, his eyes narrowing. 'But why do you
choose to live out in the sticks, I ask myself. Away from
civilisation. A young woman . . . it doesn't fit. You're full
of surprises, Elaine.'

She might have answered this time, except that he had
already moved on to see what was in the next room. At
that point, he really got a shock. The tools and materials
with which she produced her unique hand-made jewellery were laid out neatly along the work-bench her father

had built for her under the window, for maximum light.

'What .. ?' Guy fingered them one by one, looking around in amazement. On a separate table was a stack of plain white plates; there were paints, palettes, brushes, thinning fluids, varnishes, sprays. 'Is this your hobby, Elaine?'

She leaned against a wall, still laughing at him. 'I don't know why you look so astonished. That,' she said, pointing to the work-bench, 'is how I earn my living, such as it is. I make jewellery.'

'I can see that——'

'And this,' she went on, pointing to the table, 'is my hobby. Painting plates. Though I have to say I've sold plenty. They fetch quite a bit, actually.'

'I should think they do.' Guy was shaking his head now. 'Those on the wall downstairs—I thought they were antiques. They're wonderful!'

'Well, I don't know about that. But thanks for the compliment. Antiques...?' She shrugged. 'Come on, let's go down. I've got some beer in the fridge, would you like one?'

'I'd love one.' He followed her down to the kitchen, asking questions, making statements. 'You're a dark horse. Why didn't you tell me about all this? How come—why did you let me believe you were an estate agent? I thought, I assumed you'd been groomed for the business, had taken charge when——'

She shook her head, sparing him the rest of the sentence. 'There are some garden chairs in the shed out there, would you get them out? I'll bring the beer, we might as well enjoy what's left of today's sunshine.'

It was only when they were settled outside that Elaine answered all his questions, telling him about herself, her likes and dislikes and that she lived, by choice, like a hermit most of the time.

'Me, too,' he said. 'When I'm working I get totally

absorbed. Hours slip by without my noticing. Hours, even days, I told you I sometimes work through the night. I expect you'll understand how it is?'

'I understand very well. I agreed with you when you said you couldn't work in a hotel. Neither could I, there's no place like home, even if it's a temporary one! I can't tell you how delighted I was when I found this cottage, though it was in a very poor state. Dad and I fixed it up together. He wanted to buy it for me, but the landlord isn't interested in selling, for some reason.'

They talked on and on, she amused, he seeming oddly peeved by his discoveries about her. 'You deceived me, did you not? Boy, did I have the wrong impression!'

'That wasn't your fault. When I'm in that office, I'm presenting a persona. It isn't me at all.'

'So I realise. I thought you were a hard-headed businesswoman.'

'What rubbish! You had me down as the most incompetent——'

'That's not true. I thought your staff incompetent; I thought you were the big boss.'

'I am.' Her smile was rueful. 'For the moment.'

'What does that mean?'

'Well—the business, I'm not quite sure what I'm going to do with it. It's of no interest to me at all. I'm just not cut out for . . . The thing is . . .' Without stopping to think about it, Elaine found herself telling Guy all about Don Black's offer for taking over the estate agency. She told him also about the alternative: she had been approached by the directors of another, much larger concern which was also in Bury, which had been the main opposition for many years.

'What I have against their taking over is, I know, a purely emotional reaction. They've got plenty of money, but I just can't see myself allowing them to take over Dad's business, to have it swallowed up——'

'That is illogical,' Guy agreed. 'Or do you think your father would have hated the idea?'

'I simply don't know. He was only forty-seven years old. He knew I'd never follow in his footsteps, but—well, at his age why should he have thought in terms of what would happen when he retired? There again, maybe he did, but he never spoke about the long-term future, about selling up.'

Guy listened intently as she went on. He went over several points regarding Don's offer, asking her questions which made her think. At length, to her astonishment, he ended by saying almost exactly what her solicitor had said. The only difference was that Guy hadn't met Don, whereas Mr Jackson knew him quite well. 'Elaine, I obviously can't give you an opinion on the man, but it's quite clear that you like him and trust him.'

She nodded her agreement. 'Yes, to both those things.'

'And you say you're in no hurry to get full payment.'

'No. I'll have the money from the house and—I'm going to want for nothing. Dad's left me quite well off. Besides,' she shrugged, 'what do I want money for, anyway?'

Guy smiled at that. 'Let's keep to the point. I think you should follow your instincts. You don't want the business to be taken over by these other people, you do want Don to have it. Maybe you don't exactly need money, but you're damned if you're going to put at risk that which is rightly yours, what your grandfather and your father worked hard to achieve.'

Elaine looked directly at him. 'Exactly. All that. That's precisely how I feel.'

'So answer me this: is Don Black efficient? Does he know the business thoroughly? Is he likely to make a go of it, thereby fulfilling his own ambition—and being in a position to pay you off fully in time, according to the terms he's proposed?'

'Yes. Yes, I believe he can. As a matter of fact, my father had been thinking of making him a partner . . .'

She had her answer. It was what she had felt, basically, all along. But she had needed feedback from someone else. Mr Jackson and Guy Harris had arrived at the same conclusion.

'That's as far as I can go, Elaine—pointing out the advantages and disadvantages. It has to be your decision in the end.'

She was smiling. 'Thank you. I'm feeling much——' She broke off, giggling in embarrassment at the loud growling noise her stomach had just decided to make. 'Sorry about that! I'm absolutely starving, come to think of it!'

'So am I—come to think of it!'

'Really? Well, I've got a nice—*oh, my God*!' The loin chops! She'd put them in the oven with some potatoes about fifteen minutes before Guy had turned up. Without a word of explanation, she bolted from her chair, across the lawn and into a kitchen which was not exactly smoke-filled but ominously hot and smelly. Fortunately the windows were wide open. She grabbed a pair of oven-gloves and retrieved a crackling, spitting roasting tin containing a pathetic, shrivelled piece of meat and some blackened potatoes sticking tenaciously to the side of it.

'Was that our dinner?'

She turned at the sound of Guy's voice, not knowing whether to laugh or to cry. 'I'm afraid so.' She looked down at the burnt offerings. 'You wouldn't believe how big that loin was when I put it in. I was going to have some of it cold with a salad tomorrow.'

'It's my fault.'

She stuck her hands on her hips. 'It's no use standing there suppressing laughter. I can see your amusement in your eyes. I know, I know before you say it. This is no major tragedy. But I'm *starving* and I haven't got anything else to eat. That is, I mean I've got enough to see me through another month, but it's all in the *freezer*. If only I'd thought earlier——'

Guy was leaning lazily against the door, shaking his head as if in despair. 'It's all my fault,' he said again. 'I think I'll go shoot myself.'

'Will you please be serious? Do you know how far we are from the nearest shops? Not that they're open at this hour!'

'Let's make it a hanging instead. There are plenty of trees around here. Got any rope?'

'*Guy*'!

'I know for a fact there are no restaurants between Manchester and the Scottish border, so the only decent, honourable thing a man can do is——'

'*Restaurants?* Will you take a look at me?' Elaine flung out her arms in disgust. It would take her two hours to get ready for a restaurant!

His laughter was no longer suppressed. 'Take a look at you? If only you could see yourself! Two little black feet.' He mocked her, imitating her stance. 'Planted firmly apart. Green eyes flashing wickedly.'

'You idiot——'

'Hands on hips, fists clenched. And beyond this vision lies what should have been my dinner, all charcoal and rubber.'

'*Your* dinner——'

'And what does my hostess do? Shrieks at me like a fishwife.'

Elaine turned round, picked up a satisfyingly wet dish-cloth and flung it at him. It wasn't satisfying when he caught it and threw it back so fast that it landed smack in her face. 'Why, you rat! I'll——'

She got no further. Guy pounced, grabbed both her arms and held them behind her back. 'Ow! All right, all right! I take it all back. Enough!'

'Okay, lady, you've got two seconds to tell me where the eggs are kept.' When she felt a finger prodding into her back, gun-fashion, she collapsed with laughter. Guy slackened his grip but did not let go of her. In a poor imitation of James Cagney he demanded to know whether she had any cheese. Milk. Butter. Bread.

Elaine was prostrate. Her knees buckled and she half fell against him. Then his arms wrapped around her completely as he turned her round to face him.

Suddenly everything stopped, laughter, movement— and time, or so it seemed. She was hard up against him, her barely covered breasts pressing against his solid chest. Their eyes had met and now held, registering surprise if not bewilderment. A shock of desire made itself known along every inch of Elaine's body, where it was and where it wasn't in contact with his. She knew he felt it too, knew it without a doubt. For seconds they looked at one another, motionless, their breathing rapid after their struggle.

It was Guy who broke the silence, the tension of that moment. 'Okay.' He let go of her, stepped away from her. 'Why don't you go and clean up while I make us something to eat?'

'Yes, I—think I'll do that.' Elaine walked out of the kitchen at once, unquestioning. She was too shaken to think, to tell him where things were, to ask what he was going to throw together. She slipped upstairs to get a change of clothes, carried them down to the bathroom and got under the shower.

She was trembling. As she shampooed her hair, scrubbed her hands and feet, her mind was running riot. But through the chaos of her thoughts, her feelings, one thing became frighteningly clear. She would never have believed it possible; this was, for God's sake, only the second ... third ... occasion she had spent time with

Guy Harris, but—but she was falling in love with him.

'Don't be ridiculous.' Elaine said the words, aloud, but it changed nothing. 'You're attracted to him, that's all. It's just physical.'

She didn't believe that, either. There was more to it than that. Much more. Fast and furious, unbelievably, *she was falling in love with him*. What else could explain her buoyancy, the feeling that since meeting him she had walked out of fog, into sunlight? Of course it wouldn't last, it couldn't last. She didn't want it to: the price was too high.

For minutes she stood under the streaming water, panic-stricken, not knowing what she was going to do. How did one prevent oneself from falling in love?

'Elaine?' Guy's voice came booming over the sound of running water. 'Can you hear me? How long before you're ready?'

She put both hands flat against the tiled wall, trying to compose herself, to make her voice come out properly. 'Oh, give me ten minutes, would you? I want to dry my hair a little.'

'Fine.'

Upstairs in the privacy of her bedroom, Elaine tried hard to make sense of things. Guy Harris was a stranger. She knew almost nothing about him, how could she possibly be falling for him? She didn't even know where his home was, whether he even had one. Had he come from America? Would he be going back there once he had finished his new book? He had said he had no wife, but he had also said he was a family man—sort of. He was going to be in Lancashire for six, nine months. And then what? Come to think of it, she didn't even know why he had come here today.

It was over dinner that she asked him that question. She walked into the kitchen appearing fully composed, freshly scrubbed and smelling of soap, wearing a clean pair of jeans and a crisp, blue blouse. Her hair was almost dry, hanging loosely to her shoulders, and Guy's eyebrows rose in approval.

'Hello, again. Is this the real you?'

'This is the real me,' she smiled. 'Somewhere between the two extremes you've encountered before.' And what of you? she wondered. Which was the real Guy Harris, the angry man who had stormed into her office or the one who could make her laugh so easily? The one who was intense, obviously devoted to and deeply serious about his work? The man who had listened to her carefully, who'd advised her logically, who had shown genuine interest in what she did, where she lived? And why, why had he done that? Guy Harris was no ordinary person; his was virtually a household name. Yet one never saw publicity about him. He liked his privacy too much to encourage that, no doubt. But he was no introvert ... apparently.

Who are you, Guy?

How can you make me feel this way?

I don't even know you.

'Hey, I'm impressed!' She laughed delightedly, allowing none of her thoughts to intrude on what was happening. On the small kitchen table he had placed before her a steaming dish of macaroni cheese. 'Not half bad for a rooting-in-the-cupboards job!'

'My sentiments entirely.' He sat opposite her, looking pleased with himself. 'Sorry about the mess. I'm a messy cook.'

'So I see.' The draining board was stacked; he seemed to have used every pan she possessed. Of course she said nothing—his effort was more than welcome. It tasted good, too.

She remembered her manners. 'This is nice. Thank you. Now supposing you tell me what brought you here?'

'Mm?' said Guy. 'Oh, yes, I'd quite forgotten ... I'm

here to ask a favour of you. I saw Mr Prentis today—it was he who told me your address, by the way. I'm afraid I've upset your solicitor. Mr Jackson, isn't it?'

'Upset him? How? Why?' Elaine was confused.

'Didn't he call you this afternoon?'

'Not that I know of. I was in the garden most of the time, with the radio on. I might not have heard the phone ring.'

'Then I'd better explain.' Guy spread his hands, looking at her with that intensely serious expression which was becoming familiar. He was about to talk business. 'Elaine, I've explained my reasons for wanting to get settled in *Rosalie* as soon as possible. I want to keep the time I spend away from home at a minimum.'

The temptation to interrupt was enormous. Home, he'd said. Where was that? And with whom—if anyone?

'And, with your agreement,' he went on, 'there's no reason why I shouldn't move in before completion.' He smiled. 'You can imagine the solicitors' reaction to that!'

'Highly irregular, or words to that effect?'

'Exactly. And it is. Mr Prentis was astonished, insisted Mr Jackson wouldn't wear it. I had him call Mr Jackson and get a reaction. He said no. Of course it's for *you* to decide.'

She shrugged. 'As far as I'm concerned you can move in as soon as I've taken my stuff out, provided——'

'Provided you're sure of getting paid—naturally. I've given Mr Prentis a certified cheque. That placated him, of course. I dare say it's already in a bank account earning him interest until he hands it over to Mr Jackson.'

Elaine laughed. 'Where it'll earn him interest till he hands it over to me. You seem very familiar with the way solicitors work. You're quite right, they make an extra few bob when and where they can.'

Her choice of words amused him. 'Few bob. And why

not? Perks of the job. They're a breed unto themselves; I should know, my father was a lawyer. A very shrewd businessman, too, of a calibre——'

This time, she did interrupt. 'Was? Is he retired?'

'Dead. Both my parents. I read law for a while, too, at Harvard.'

'Harvard!' Elaine had heard of Harvard University. 'Why—what happened? Why only for "a while"?'

'I'm a drop-out. My father was not pleased, I can tell you. All that money on fees, and I dropped out to concentrate on writing. The "risky business of", as my father put it. But it had always been my over-riding interest; I've been scribbling since I was old enough to hold a pen and——' Guy broke off. 'And we're digressing again. You're very easy to talk to, you know.'

She didn't know. At least, coming from him, it was a surprise to her.

'Elaine? I have your agreement?'

Mr Jackson would advise her against this, she knew, but Mr Prentis was holding a certified cheque and she had the final say. In any case, she trusted Guy. 'Yes, of course.'

'If you could make a start this weekend, that would be great. I'd offer to help you, but I have to go away for the weekend. Will you be able to cope alone?'

She hardly heard the last question. Away, again? Why?

'Elaine?'

'Sorry. I—was just thinking. Now let me see, I'll be visiting customers tomorrow and Saturday—I've got some deliveries to make, they're urgent. I can clear out the small stuff from the house on Sunday, but I'll need a van for the bits of furniture I'm taking. That means I can't clear everything until Monday. How's that?'

He was obviously pleased. 'Then I will be able to help, after all. I'll get back from Cornwall on Sunday night.'

'Cornwall?'—she said it lightly, casually. 'Is that where you live?'

There was a slight hesitation, only slight. 'I have a house there. Where I *live* is—yet to be decided.'

It was as far as she dared go, something was telling her not to push her luck. 'Well, supposing you meet me at *Rosalie* at two o'clock on Monday. I must spend the morning in the office—tell Don he can have the business. So I'll be at the house at two, with a van. You can do the lifting.'

'Sounds fair,' grinned Guy. 'You're not exactly built for lifting things, are you?'

When his eyes started to rove over her, she picked up their empty plates and moved to the sink. 'All I can offer for afters is some ice cream. Okay?'

'Not for me. I'm full.'

So was she. 'Then we'd better tackle this lot.' She looked at the draining board, laughing to herself. How had he managed to make such a mess? 'I'll wash, you wipe.'

There was the click of his cigarette lighter, followed by low laughter. 'You must be joking. *I* produced dinner. *You* clear up. Let me know when coffee's ready.'

Elaine turned, aghast. 'What a nerve! I think the least——'

But he had gone.

When she emerged with a pot of freshly-brewed coffee, having washed up in the meantime, it was to find Guy lying on the two-seater settee, smoking, looking up at the ceiling, miles away. She had to force herself not to laugh. His bulk more than filled the width of it, his knees were draped over one arm.

'Move, you big overgrown oaf. *I* made the coffee, *you* can pour it. One sugar, lots of milk for me. And may I have a cigarette, please?'

'Didn't realise you smoked.'

'I like one occasionally. I always smoke when I'm stressed. Like now.'

'Are you really?' She had the benefit of that slow, gorgeous smile of his.

'No, I'm lying. Just trying to make you feel guilty.'

'If there's one thing I dislike, it's manipulative women.'

'Then it's just as well I'm not your type, isn't it?'

He seemed surprised at that. 'Who said?'

'You did.'

'I never said any such thing. Maybe I gave that impression—but I didn't know you at the time.'

'You still don't.'

'I know enough to realise you're not really manipulative.'

'That would be a difficult thing to achieve with you.' He hadn't moved. It was she who was pouring the coffee, moving a side table nearer the settee.

'Elaine?' The tone of his voice brought her eyes immediately to his. 'Tell me more. You interest me. I want to know more about you.'

He meant it. But what else could she tell him? He practically knew her life story as it was. She had told him about leaving home, about her years learning her craft in college, her need for independence, how she came to find this cottage and how she loved living here alone . . . or used to.

In the face of her silence, he asked, 'Is there a man in your life? If not, why not?'

She sat, discomfited by the questions. She had never met anyone like Guy before, had never been in love. No, that wasn't true. She'd thought herself in love twice in the past. *Thought* herself. Maybe—maybe what she felt for Guy Harris would be transitory, would pass as those other feelings had passed. She hoped so. Once he was settled in her parents' house, it would be the end of their association, wouldn't it? The very idea depressed her.

'I'm sorry.' Guy pulled himself into a sitting position. 'I was trespassing on your privacy. I hate that. I didn't mean——'

'Oh, it's all right.' She waved an arm. 'I have no secrets in that respect. No, there isn't a man in my life. I simply don't feel the need. I'm very self-sufficient. Haven't you noticed?'

'Yes. But it doesn't seem——' He paused, looking at her, ordering his thoughts before he went on. 'Am I to take it you live a celibate life, Elaine?'

To her chagrin she felt a blush suffusing her face. Oh, it was all too easy to see how his mind was working. This was something she had to cope with from many people: her parents when they were alive, her friends; even Don Black had hinted at the 'peculiarity' of her life-style, probably because she didn't fancy him and had made it clear. She lowered her eyes, unsure how to answer Guy, unsure whether to try. Would he, could he understand if she explained it to him? Probably not. 'Now you've gone too far,' she said quietly. 'It's really none of——'

'My business? Oh, come on, we've gone past that stage. Don't close up on me now. You just told me I wasn't trespassing, that you had no secrets in this respect. So tell me. Talk to me. *Communicate*.'

Communicate. Communication was his business, wasn't it? A writer had to know people, to understand people thoroughly. Was his interest, therefore, general rather than personal? In any case, what the hell? They were, were they not, ships that passed in the night? She answered him honestly, hesitantly at first. 'Yes. I find it—well, I find it irritating how people, even my own parents, always try to categorise other people. There's nothing strange about me, if that's what you're thinking.'

'The idea never entered my head, Elaine. Don't think I'm guilty of labelling you, categorising you. Because you live a little differently it doesn't mean you're an outcast from society, or abnormal.'

'Society!' Elaine leaned forward, all hesitation gone. 'That's the problem. We're brought up to expect a certain life-style, to expect other people to expect it, and to expect it of us, to behave in a certain way. If someone deviates, like a young man marrying an older woman— the reverse being acceptable, within reason of course—it causes a ripple—gossip, speculation. Likewise if people of two different classes marry: problems. For both families respectively. They wonder how they're going to cope, to bridge the barriers. With me it's a different kind of deviation from the norm. I do go out occasionally, with people of my own age, but for most of the time I live like a hermit and no, there's no man in my life. Even more puzzling to people is the fact that I'm not looking for one. I'm twenty-two, and while nowadays people are sufficiently enlightened not to expect automatically that I'm itching to get married and have babies, they do at least *expect* me to have a sex life. Well, I'm perfectly content as I am. Why can't people accept that, believe it?'

'You've already answered that question.'

Elaine nodded, shrugging. 'When I feel the need, if I do, I'll go out and find myself a lover.'

'That won't present any problem.' His smile was fleeting. 'Lover, you said. Have you anything against marriage? No, don't look at me like that. I heard all you said, but it's a fair question.'

And so it was. 'Okay. Then let me add this: if I feel the need for marriage, I'll go out and find myself a husband.'

'Now you're being flippant.'

'Of course I am. Finding a lover and finding someone with whom you want to live and share the rest of your life are very different. The former can be done with a certain amount of detachedness, cold calculation. All you need is the spark of physical attraction.'

Guy was quiet for a moment before asking, 'And finding a husband? What ingredients are necessary for marriage?'

Elaine knew what he expected her to say. She laughed, shaking her head. 'Now there's a loaded question! You think I'm going to walk into that trap? You expect I'll say the obvious—love.'

'And won't you?'

Elaine shifted slightly. He was watching her, his grey eyes impassive, merely interested—but there was a smile tugging at his lips. 'Not the fairytale kind. Obviously there needs to be ... fondness and respect. As a minimum. More importantly, in my opinion, there has to be compatibility. I have a girl-friend, someone who was in my class at school, same age as I. She fell head over heels in love when she was eighteen. You never saw anything like it: walking on cloud nine she was, sparkling with it! She said she had only just started to live. Her boy-friend was in a similar state. They married, at eighteen, and were separated within six months. They're divorced now, needless to say. They had nothing in common. What a way to find out!'

'What should they have done?'

'They should have waited before marrying—found out before the event, not after.'

'It sounds to me as if you've never been in love.'

Elaine groaned inwardly. This conversation was becoming ... awkward. 'Actually, I have. At least—I thought I was. It wore off.'

'You make it sound like an illness,' he remarked.

'Well, I certainly don't think it helps people to think clearly!'

'That I will go along with.'

It was only in the ensuing silence that she realised how cleverly he had drawn her out, got her talking without volunteering anything himself. 'And you, Guy? I think

I'm entitled to a question now. You told me you have no wife but—are you married, in fact?'

'No. Good grief, did you think I'd lied?'

'You could have had an estranged wife.'

'Who would still be a wife. I'm a widower, Elaine.' He reached for the coffee pot, asking her if she'd like a refill.

Elaine said no, and she was not going to be put off, to let him change the subject. This was too important to her. In spite of all she had paid lip-service to, her protestations about the way people are conditioned, she could not deny the relief she had felt on hearing he was free. She was already worried over the way she felt about him; to discover she was falling in love with a married man would have unnerved her. There were some conventional codes of behaviour she adhered to and agreed with wholeheartedly. 'And you were in love with your wife when you married her?'

He was busy with the coffee pot, not looking at her. His answer was short, his voice tight. 'Madly.'

She couldn't go on. Guy was a widower, not a divorcee. She wouldn't risk digging further when this was different, when in his case it would obviously hurt him to tell her more. Besides, she didn't really want to hear more. So it was she who changed the subject. 'About manipulation. Joking aside, have you ever stopped to think about how much we—people, I mean—manipulate one another?'

He laughed at that. 'It's something I've thought about in depth, as a matter of fact . . .'

It was only when the clock on her mantelpiece struck yet again that Elaine actually looked at it. It had struck the hour several times and they had been too deep in conversation actually to register the time. 'Guy, it's midnight!'

'So?'

'So I have to get up in the morning.'

'Why, Elaine, how boring of you! You disappoint me. I thought you were enjoying yourself. I know I am.'

'I am! But——' But what? She probably wouldn't get to sleep in any case. Even now, she realised, he was going to keep her awake for hours—whether he stayed longer or not. 'You're right. In that case, I'll make some fresh coffee. I hope instant will do?'

'Have you got anything to drink—I mean *drink* drink?'

'I'm sorry, Guy, I haven't. It's something I never think about unless I'm——' she broke off laughing. 'Unless I'm *expecting* company.'

'Message received and understood,' he smiled. 'I shall call and warn you next time—and bring a bottle.'

Next time? Was there going to be a next time?

It was ten minutes to three when he left. With an apology. 'Hey, I'm sorry, I must go.' He stood up, stretching, his hands touching the ceiling as he did so. 'You're falling asleep on the spot.'

'I'm—yes, I am tired.' Elaine got to her feet—almost. She had spent the past hour sitting with one leg tucked under her. Her foot had gone to sleep; when she put it on the floor, her leg gave way.

'Steady!' Guy's arm came around her waist.

Elaine's breath caught as his hand brushed against her breast. 'I'm all right. I—my foot's gone to sleep.'

'I realised that.' He kept his arm around her, smiling down at her, making her heart thump so violently she feared he would hear it. She looked away, avoiding his eyes even when he spoke her name. 'Elaine?' It came out softly, very softly.

Why couldn't she look at him? He was going to kiss her, she didn't doubt that for a second. Why was the prospect as frightening as it was longed for?

'I see.' Still his voice was soft. But he didn't see. He let go of her, saying something about seeing her on Monday afternoon.

When Elaine saw him out into the blackness of the night, she stood limply against her closed front door, listening to the sound of the Porsche's powerful engine as he drove away, cursing herself for her reluctance, a reluctance he had read implicitly. Of course he had. He was a sensitive man, attuned to her to an extraordinary extent in spite of their short acquaintance.

Attuned, as she was to him.

CHAPTER THREE

FOR almost two hours Elaine was packing boxes on Sunday, making the trip from the house to her car and back again. She had had time in which to get used to the idea of saying goodbye to *Rosalie* once and for all; tonight would be the last time she would sleep in the house, to be handy for the office in the morning. Yet the task of collecting the things she couldn't part with saddened her enormously. Photographs, ornaments, her mother's jewellery.

Her parents' clothes, still hanging in their wardrobes, were her first task. She put them all in big plastic bags, every last item, and put them in the hall. She would take them to the Oxfam shop in Bury tomorrow.

She left until last the sorting of things she didn't know whether she wanted to keep—like the contents of the bookcases. It was then that she came across three books written by Guy. Which of her parents had read them? Maybe they both had. Foolishly, irrelevantly, she found herself hoping this was so. Would they have liked Guy, had they met him? She felt sure they would. Inside the front covers of the books she looked for the date of their publication—ten, nine and two years ago respectively. So two of them were examples of his earlier work. His earliest, perhaps? She had no way of knowing. One of the older titles was very familiar; it had been made into a television series. Alas, she hadn't watched it. Well, she would make up for that. She would read everything Guy Harris had written to date, she couldn't wait to. As if hoarding a secret and precious cache she put the books in to the glove compartment of her car, promising she would start one as soon as she got home.

She started with the earliest, and it came as a rude awakening to her. Reading Guy's work was like living inside someone else's head; one was not aware that one was reading at all. His attraction for the reader, his gift, was understandable, appreciated, by the very first page. Elaine was hooked. What she had hitherto thought would not be her type of entertainment became, within the space of a half-hour, compulsive reading. She had started with *MacKinlay & Sons*, a novel set in Guy's native America, in New England, beginning in the latter half of the nineteenth century and spanning sixty years. She read until her eyes wouldn't stay open any longer, was left in suspense, annoyed because she simply had to sleep.

Sleep. It came quickly that night, with thoughts of the family about whom she had been reading, their problems, the complexity of the inter-relationships. Marvellous stuff. But how could Guy know, how could he be so accurate with the characterisation of Molly, an eighteen-year-old female? And her sister Blanche, twenty-nine and on the shelf, frustrated and afraid of the future; their grandfather, eighty-two and as wise as God in his family's eyes? Guy had painted them all vividly, bringing them to life as though they really existed. And the plot—where had he dreamt that up? How did he get his ideas? Elaine drifted into sleep with a smile on her lips. The questions, the predictable questions he was always asked by people—that was probably one of them.

At nine o'clock on Monday morning she was in her father's office. No, it was Don's office now. Don's business. Elaine had just told him of her decision and he held out his hand, beaming his pleasure. His pleasure and, she realised, his relief.

'I'm sorry to have kept you waiting for an answer, Don. I've been so woolly of late. I—you know, I hadn't been able to think clearly until these past——'

He was shaking her hand, grinning from ear to ear. 'I know. You won't regret it, Elaine! Your faith in me is not misplaced, you'll see.'

'Don, I don't doubt that for one minute. Good luck to you.' She paused. 'And now what? You know I don't want to stay around. Will you employ someone else? You've got your own ideas, I suppose?'

'Yes indeed. I've got someone in mind. Someone with experience. He's fully qualified, too, a chartered survey-or. Look, don't misunderstand me, but if you want to clear out today, it's all right.'

'I don't misunderstand, Don. This—well, this is it.' She looked around the office, at the big desk which had been her father's and his father's before him. 'It's the end of . . . it's your business now. I shall leave it to you and Mr Jackson to draw up the agreement, get it all legal and set out on paper.'

Don was nodding. 'Absolutely. But we must celebrate.' Some of his effervescence disappeared. 'Will you, Elaine? Will you have dinner with me—by way of celebration?'

She almost felt sorry for him then. He liked her very much, she realised, and it had nothing to do with ulterior motives. There were none now.

'This is a champagne occasion,' he went on. 'Say yes, please!'

'Yes,' she smiled. 'Of course it is and of course I will. You say when and where.'

'Right! First off, you will dress up to the nines. We'll go somewhere swish. I shall collect you from your home. No arguments. I'll be in a taxi, blow the expense! You'll be delivered home likewise.'

Elaine was grinning. 'I see—a boozy do. Are you trustworthy, Don Black?'

'Unfortunately, yes.' He looked at her levelly. 'I think

you're well aware that my interest in you goes beyond business, Elaine.'

'Ah, well,' she said lightly, 'you can't win 'em all.'

He let it go at that. 'We should have another get together, with Pamela and Keith and Peter. I'd like to introduce the new chap to you, too. Why don't we do something here? Say—Friday. No, that's rent night. What about Thursday? Here, after we close, just a drink or two?'

'Done.'

'But our celebration, yours and mine, will be in private. Let's make it tonight. Why not?'

'Let's make it tomorrow,' she said, still in a light vein. 'This afternoon I'm meeting Guy Harris at the house. I've got to go and hire a van, don't know what time I'll be free. Guy's helping me move out the pieces of furniture I want to keep.'

'Guy Harris!' Don was shaking his head. 'I still can't believe it. Fancy selling your house to *the* Guy Harris! Have you read any of his stuff? My favourite was one set in Cornwall, now what was it called . . .?'

'*Another Time, Another Life.*' That was the one published two years ago. 'I've got it at home; I haven't started it yet.'

'It's marvellous. I wish I'd met our Mr Harris, I'd love to ask him where he gets his ideas from.'

Elaine suppressed a grin. 'You can. I'll ask him to our little shindig on Thursday, if that's all right with you.' After all, she wanted to add, but didn't, he's partly responsible for your happiness right now.

'*All right?*' Don was delighted. 'I'm honoured!'

Elaine didn't hang around. She had too much to do, had yet to make that trip to the Oxfam shop. She fixed a time for the following evening with Don and left the offices of Faraday & Faraday, which name Don would continue to use, feeling sad and happy at the same time.

She got to *Rosalie* at half past two. Guy was waiting for her, was sitting in his car on the drive. He leapt out and opened the door of the van as Elaine rolled up—coming to a very jerky halt.

She was frustrated, unable to get the hang of the vehicle's clutch—her own car was automatic. She took one look at Guy's face and held up both hands. 'Don't! I don't want any wisecracks about kangaroo petrol, women drivers or anything else. The clutch on that thing is vicious, I tell you, vicious!'

'Now would I?' He was all innocence. 'The only remark I'll make is that you should have let me hire it.'

'You mean drive it here?'

'I mean drive it here.'

'Well, blow you! You can drive it to my place.'

'I was hoping you'd say that.'

'See how you cope with the clutch. And you can take it back whence it came!'

'Anything else? Have you quite finished taking your frustrations out on me? I'll have you know I've been waiting for you for forty minutes. We said two o'clock.'

'Sorry,' she muttered. 'I tried to get here on time. There were all those forms to fill in at the van-hire place——'

Guy draped an arm around her shoulders. 'Come on, let's get to it, no need to look so down in the mouth!'

It didn't take long to load the van, to vacuum and to stick some washing in the machine—the bed linen she had used. Guy's linen now. The house was ready for him to move in to.

They drove to Elaine's cottage, unloaded and went back to *Rosalie* to pick up her car, which she drove to the van hire office so she could drive Guy home again. She had left him to drive the wretched van, which was probably illegal because she hadn't named him as a second driver. When it was all over, she was exhausted. The washing machine had long since finished by the time they got back to the house and it was as much as she could do to hang the stuff on the clothes line.

'I'll leave the ironing of this lot to you.' She grinned at Guy, watching her from the kitchen doorway. 'It's all yours now.'

There was no witty retort. He was just looking at her, frowning, against the glare of the sun, she supposed. Silently he went inside. Elaine joined him in the kitchen. The kettle was on. 'I've just realised why I've run out of energy. I haven't had a thing to eat today. Is there any food in the house?'

'How would I know?' He had his back to her, was standing with both hands on the edge of the sink, his shoulders hunched.

'Guy, what is it? What's wrong?'

Seconds passed before he turned to face her. When he did so his face had cleared, his expression was normal again. 'Nothing. Forgive me if I sounded curt. Let's have a cup of coffee, clean ourselves up a bit and go out, get ourselves a decent meal.'

'Agreed!'

Something had depressed him, some thought, some memory had been triggered, but she didn't pursue it—she wouldn't get anywhere if she did. They had a bar meal in a nearby pub, lingering afterwards over a couple of drinks, and talking as avidly as they had at their last meeting. Time flew when she was with Guy. He was so interesting to be with. Elaine didn't want to part from him now, as she hadn't wanted him to leave her the last time. They walked back to *Rosalie,* talking but not touching, and came to a halt by her car.

'You're not coming in?' Guy reached out, his fingers brushing lightly over the black silkiness of her hair.

'No, I—it's getting late.'

He stopped what he was doing, shoved both hands into the pockets of his jeans. 'When will I see you again?'

The little party on Thursday—she had forgotten about it. Should she ask Guy? Did he want to see her again or was he merely being polite? There was only one way to find out. 'Do you want to?'

'Would I have asked the question if I didn't? I'm not in the habit of saying things I don't mean. You should realise that by now.'

Why should she, when he knew her far better than she knew him? This man was expert at directing conversation, at putting up shields when it came to talking about himself. She told him about the get-together on Thursday, that Don would like to meet him. 'I more or less promised you'd be there, actually. Do you mind?'

'That depends. In what capacity?'

Laughter bubbled out of her. 'Celebrity! Sorry about that! Don and Pamela—they're both itching to talk to you. You've already met Pam, of course . . . Hmm. Well, when she learned who you are she almost had a fit. She's read *everything* you've had published, couldn't *believe* she hadn't recognised you when you came in that day!'

Guy was laughing in spite of himself. At her. 'You funny creature. Okay, I'll be there. But that's Thursday, what about tomorrow, you and me?'

'I'm going out with Don tomorrow.' She saw his eyebrows go up and put him right at once. 'Forget that. It's a celebration for him, pure and simple.'

'Has it got to be private?'

'I—well, yes, I think so, Guy. It is private, really.'

'Fair enough. I'll respect that.'

Elaine hesitated, hoping he would suggest Wednesday. He didn't. 'Well . . . goodnight. I'll ring you to make arrangements for Thursday.' She turned away, was reaching for the door handle on her car.

'Not so fast.' Guy's arms came around her from behind, turning her to face him. It happened quickly, his mouth coming down on hers, his hand holding her chin firmly, as though he were convinced she would try to pull away. The idea never occurred to her: his kiss drove all coherent thought from her mind. Her lips parted willingly beneath his, her arms closing tightly around him because it was the only natural thing to do. Never, never had she responded to a man like this before, never had she known such arousal, it was immediate, overwhelming. She slid her hands into the thick curls of his hair, realising only then how much she had been longing to do just that.

Guy's mouth moved along her face, her throat, came to rest by her ear as he spoke softly to her. 'Are you very sure you won't come in?

She did pull away then, remembering where they were, annoyed by his assumption. Her face was flushed, her breathing rapid, her green eyes sparkling with excitement and with annoyance. 'Well! You don't pull your punches, do you? One kiss and you think I'm ready to go to bed with you?'

He was looking at her the way he had on the day they'd met, giving her the feeling that he could read her mind. 'Yes, I do. That's exactly what I think. Why so indignant? You want me.'

For the life of her, she couldn't think what to say. *Did* she want him, to that extent?

'What's the matter?' he persisted. 'Isn't this the girl who likes to do as she pleases, who resents the dictates of society, conditioning? The girl who said that when she feels the need for a lover, she'll go out and find one?'

Oh, God! Something inside her recoiled. How very nicely she had cornered herself! She had said that, all of it. 'It—this is—it isn't like that.' Embarrassed, she tried to escape, to turn away from him.

His laughter made things worse, but it was fleeting. 'Hey, come here. Look at me. I said *look* at me.'

When she did he was merely smiling at her, a different

sort of smile. His eyes were gentle on her, teasing. Then he took her in his arms and held her, a gesture that had no sexuality about it this time. 'Don't let's part on a bad note. Listen to me for a moment.' He held her away from him now, looking down at her. 'You're very young, Elaine. I find you delightful ... and attractive. Very attractive. Your ideas and your way of looking at life are interesting and in many ways admirable but they're not wholly realistic.'

'I—don't know what you mean, Guy.'

'No. But if we continue to see one another, you soon will. Goodnight, Elaine.'

Inevitably his words kept her awake that night. His words and the speed with which she had fallen in love with him. There was no doubt about it now, she was sunk.

Or was she? Was there a chance that—that what? He had said he found her 'delightful and attractive'. Was that all? Why was he pursuing her, now their business was as good as finished? If 'pursuing' was the right word. Yes, it was. It was he who had suggested meeting again, before she had mentioned Thursday's get-together in the office.

She turned over restlessly in bed, curling into a ball as if to protect herself from Guy and all the uncertainty he made her feel. It hurt. Had she felt like this when she had been in love before? If so, she couldn't remember.

Things got worse for her. The small party in the office was successful and pleasant; if Guy was bothered by all the questions he was asked, he didn't show it. Afterwards, when he walked with her to her car, he explained that he never did show impatience. How could he, why should he, when people were showing an interest in him? 'It would be arrogant in the extreme not to respond,' he said. 'People would misunderstand. On the other hand, I don't go looking for evenings such as this.'

'I know, I'm sorry, I realise you're a very private person. It was sweet of you to indulge me—and them. I can't help it,' she added lightly, 'I'm rather proud of you, you know.'

He didn't answer that. Nor did he kiss her, except by raising her hand to his lips. 'Goodnight, lovely girl. I'll be in touch.'

Elaine watched, her heart thumping with something approaching panic as he turned and walked in the direction of his car. He'd be in touch. When? And would he, really?

A week went by, days during which Elaine became more and more distracted. Guy was constantly on her mind. She worked solidly, as much as she was able to creatively and then afterwards on more mundane things. Since she had moved the extra furniture into the cottage, *it* was overcrowded. Why hadn't she thought of that? The place was too small to accommodate anything over and above what she already had. As it was, she had a bookcase in the kitchen, a box full of things in the garden shed and a set of coffee tables stacked in the tiny hall, making use of the front door impossible. But she had been unable to part with those tables; they had been a wedding present to her parents, from her grandparents. They were beautiful, inlaid rosewood, an example of craftsmanship rarely seen nowadays.

It was the beginning of August when Guy phoned her, apologising for his absence and explaining that he had been busy getting the house organised. 'How about spending the day with me tomorrow?'

It was all she could do to hide her relief, her joy. 'Aren't you working on your book yet?'

'Lord, yes. I'm well into it. That's the main reason I haven't been in touch. But I have to drive over to Yorkshire tomorrow to do some research. I thought you might be interested, might like to come with me.'

'Okay,' she said casually. 'Why not? They've forecast a beautiful day.'

They had got it wrong! Guy picked her up at eight the following morning and it was raining cats and dogs. Nevertheless, it was a beautiful day as far as Elaine was concerned. Guy certainly appeared to enjoy it, too. They drove, they spent time in libraries, a museum, talking to people he had arranged to meet, people who could help him. They had lunch and, rather late, dinner on the way back. It was after ten when he delivered Elaine home. And it was still raining. He saw her to her door—the back door, remarking how crazy it was and that she should have left the extra furniture at *Rosalie* until such time as he put it on the market. It would have made no difference in the long run, though, as she pointed out. 'Sooner or later I'd have ended up with more stuff than I need.'

'Perhaps you'd better find a bigger home.'

'Certainly not!' she laughed. 'I'll cope.'

He refused her offer of coffee. He saw her safely inside and left at once. 'No, thanks. No coffee. I have to get to work.'

'Now? But it'll be almost midnight before you're home.'

'I've told you, I work when the mood takes me. Goodnight, Elaine.'

Goodnight, Elaine. She felt bereft. Not even so much as a kiss on the hand this time!

Nor was there during the following few weeks. Guy phoned her, often, and when he was doing research they spent full days together. Otherwise they got together for a few hours at lunchtime, or an evening, always at her place or out somewhere. She hadn't actually set foot in *Rosalie* since the day she had moved all her things out. The contract on the sale had been signed, completion effected.

Elaine was and was not feeling on top of the world throughout the whole of August. Guy was very attentive, always arriving with a gift, chocolates or flowers or wine and so on. Yet physically he deliberately kept his distance. It was this more than anything else that puzzled her. He didn't even *attempt* to seduce her. Of course she had more food for thought than that alone—plenty of it. There were so many questions still unanswered. It had reached the stage where she knew the man, or at least she thought so, but not his history.

It wasn't until the middle of September that Elaine got the answers to those questions, that he trusted her, finally, with the facts regarding his circumstances: his past, his present and his future.

CHAPTER FOUR

IT was when Guy phoned her on a Saturday morning that Elaine was alerted to the change which was about to take place in their relationship. She had never seen him during a weekend, and rarely on a Friday. She knew he went away. He never mentioned it now, he didn't need to. Sometimes he left town on a Friday, sometimes early Saturday. So when he phoned her from *Rosalie* early one Saturday morning, she guessed what was coming.

'Just checking that you're in,' he was saying. 'I'm at home. Is it okay for me to come over?'

'Certainly. Come in time for lunch.'

There was a pause. 'I—thought I'd come earlier than that. Around ten. And ... Elaine, I won't be alone. There's someone I want you to meet.'

She knew. She had known, somehow, for a long time. 'That's fine. I'll be delighted. See you when I see you.' No questions, this was not the time to ask. He would tell her, soon, all that she wanted to know.

She was in her work-room when Guy arrived with his child. It was a boy. She had wondered. A boy, about four years old if she were not mistaken. What did she know about children? From the upstairs window she watched, a little nervously, as the man and the boy approached the house. She headed for the stairs, praying that she would cope as she wanted to cope. Even at a distance the resemblance between them was striking. When she was actually face to face with the child, she thought it uncanny; even if she had not been prepared, he would have needed no introduction as Guy's son. The grey eyes, the mop of thick black hair—he was Guy Harris in miniature.

'Hello.' Elaine spoke first, smiling her welcome at the kitchen door just as Guy opened it. 'I've been waiting to meet you, young man; I'm glad you've come to see me.'

'Hello.' The child held out his hand quite formally. 'I'm James, but everyone calls me Jamie. I'm four and a quarter.'

'How do you do?' She shook his hand, following his lead. 'I'm Elaine. I'm twenty-two and three quarters.'

It was only then that she allowed herself to look at Guy. Their eyes met and held, hers full of accusation she couldn't hide. Why? Why wait till now? If you couldn't bring him, you could at least have told me about him.

And in his eyes, the answer. I'm sorry. Really, I'm sorry. I'll explain. Give me time.

'We've got a surprise for you!' Jamie was saying. 'It's something you don't know about. We haven't brought it with us.'

'It's nothing exciting, I'm afraid.' Guy ushered the child inside, his hand reaching for and briefly squeezing Elaine's as they all trooped in to the living room. 'Just the contents of the loft at *Rosalie*. You didn't think about looking up there, did you?'

'I didn't know there was anything in the loft——'

'Three boxes!' Jamie informed her. 'They're all tied up with string and Daddy wouldn't let me open them. He said it might be private.'

Elaine looked at the child. She knew where his intelligence came from. Had his mother been bright, too? He was still going on about the mysterious boxes. 'What's in them, Elaine?' he asked excitedly.

'I've no idea. But I'll tell you if it's anything exciting.'

'Promise?'

'Promise!'

He thought a moment. 'That means I'll be seeing you

again! I'm glad! I like you.'

'Jamie, you don't even know me!'

'That doesn't matter, I know I like you. Can I come again, next time Daddy brings me to his other house?'

'Of course you can, I'd be very disappointed if you didn't.'

His attention shifted; he was standing by the window which overlooked the back garden, had spotted the pond in it. 'Are there any fish in that pond?'

Elaine moved to his side and opened the French window. 'Why don't you go and see? When Jamie raced away, she turned to face his father. 'Why?' she asked softly.

'I'm—not really sure.'

'That's no answer!'

'I realise that. But it's the truth.' He lowered himself in to a chair, the tension in his body apparent to her.

'It doesn't matter. I'd guessed anyway.'

'I know. But it does matter. Sit down, Elaine.'

'I can't. I want to keep an eye on Jamie—the pond's deep enough to be dangerous to a four-year-old.'

'What is this? The emergence of a maternal instinct?'

She looked at him. 'Perhaps. He's a lovely child, Guy.'

'Thank you. I think so, too, but I can't take all the credit.'

'Who looks after him? Where does he live?'

'In Cornwall. With his grandparents at the moment.'

His wife's parents. He'd told her his parents were dead.

'I—must go and do things in the kitchen. Do go out to him, Guy.'

He was already on his feet. Unbeknown to them she watched them for a moment, Guy bending and taking hold of his son's hand, Jamie pointing at the fish, counting them by the look of it. There was a sudden constriction in her chest. She knew, now, why it hurt so much. She wasn't merely in love; she loved. And this was a first. She loved Guy Harris in a way she had never loved anyone before—as a woman loves a man.

It was a successful visit. Guy and Jamie stayed till the late afternoon and Elaine's prayers were answered. She had coped as she had hoped to, even better than. Jamie had made it easy, though. He was interested in everything around him, in her and the things in the cottage, was fascinated by her work-room. When they were leaving he extracted another promise from her, one she made happily.

'Elaine, next time I visit can I paint one of those plates like you do? Will you show me how? Is it hard?'

'Yes, yes and—well, let's say there's a knack to it.'

'A knack?' He looked to his father for interpretation.

'What Elaine means is that it requires a great deal of talent to do it properly.'

Jamie nodded. He knew what talent meant.

'I'll see you on Tuesday,' Guy told her. 'I'm driving Jamie back to Cornwall tomorrow, I'll be back late Monday evening. Do you want me to bring those boxes here?'

'No, that's okay. I'm going in to Bury on Tuesday afternoon. I want to do some shopping and see how Don's getting on. I'll come to your house when I've finished, if that's all right with you.'

'Of course!' He seemed inordinately pleased. 'I've been under the impression you didn't want to go in there again.'

'Not at all. It won't bother me any more.'

Nor did it. On the following Tuesday she walked in to *Rosalie* without a qualm. She was in for a shock. The house was not merely untidy, it was chaotic. Scattered around the floor of the living room were stacks of books, more books, magazines, records. There were several empty glasses lying around, several pairs of shoes and several ashtrays—all overflowing.

'Good God in heaven!' Elaine exclaimed. 'What is this?'

Guy didn't seem to know what she meant. 'What's what?'

She couldn't help laughing at him. 'This—this *pig mess*!'

'Oh.' He followed her gaze, shrugging. 'I suppose you're right.'

The kitchen was as bad. 'Guy, if you must live out of tins—*cans*, as you Americans call them—you might at least put them in the rubbish when you've emptied them!'

He repeated what she'd said, word for word, mocking her mercilessly.

'Okay, so I'm a nag. You need a housekeeper.'

'I know it,' he admitted.

'What's the upstairs like?'

'Come and see.'

It wasn't too bad. What had been Elaine's room was now Jamie's—for his visits. There were two teddy bears and other tell-tale signs that this was now a child's domain. What had been her parents' room was now Guy's and what had been the guest bedroom was now his study. In it was a vast desk housing a word processor, a printer, reams of paper, pens and other such paraphernalia. Again there were ashtrays dotted about—overflowing, of course, and more empty glasses and mugs. She turned to him. 'You know that big white thing in the corner in the kitchen? It's called a dishwasher.'

'A what?'

'A——' She poked him in the ribs. 'How come you chose to work in here? There's a study downstairs.'

'This room's bigger. The downstairs study is now the spare bedroom-cum-boxroom. Speaking of which——'

The boxes! She'd forgotten about them.

'I blew the dust off them,' Guy went on, 'and stuck them in the empty wardrobe in my room. If they turn out to be a load of junk, I'll put them out with the trash.'

'I've no doubt it will be a load of junk. What made you go exploring in the loft, by the way?'

'Jamie. He spotted the trap door in the ceiling—you can imagine the rest.'

'Curiosity?'

'A trap door is irresistible to a four-year-old.'

Was it? It was another reminder of how little she knew about children. She sat down in the armchair in the corner of Guy's study. He sat by his desk, noticing at once the change of expression on her face. 'Elaine, you've got to forgive me. I still can't answer your question. Not really, not satisfactorily. I—think I wanted to get to know you better before I told you about Jamie. Or rather, I wanted you to get to know me better. I—didn't want to put you off, I suppose.'

'Put me off?'

'Me. You might have lost interest had you known I had a child.'

Could he know, could he guess, how much those words pleased her? She hoped not. She paused before answering him, schooling her face and her voice to neutrality. 'I find that very odd. Surely you realise I've wanted to know more about you? After all, I think you know everything there is to know about me. Guy, why don't you tell me, just *tell me* about yourself!' Her composure had slipped. 'Trust me! For heaven's sake, trust me! If it makes any difference at all, I'll feel——' She broke off. Careful, be careful, Elaine. 'I mean—well, I can only feel flattered if you'll trust me.'

'Trust? Oh, Elaine! It isn't a matter of trust, it's——' Guy stood, his fingers raking through the black mass of his hair. 'My life's in a mess, an unholy mess!'

She waited in silence, tense, anxious and trying not to

show it, until he could open up to her. Very quietly she said, 'Start at the beginning, Guy. Please.'

It was seconds before he spoke; he was just looking at her, not really seeing her. 'The beginning.' He reached for the cigarettes on his desk and sat down again. 'My wife, Helen, was English. Cornish to be more precise. I—we met in Florida, she was over there on holiday with two girl friends. She was twenty-three, she'd finished university a year earlier. I was the same age, I'd dropped out of Harvard and had moved to Florida three years earlier. My parents and most of my family were living in New York—that's where I was born. I wanted to get away from cities, to live alone and concentrate on writing. In spite of his disapproval, when my father realised how serious I was he bought me the house in Florida and wished me good luck.

'I'd had my first book published and another one accepted when I met Helen. We met on the beach one afternoon when . . . that's hardly relevant, is it? We—it was one of those love at first sight things. It does happen, though I'd never believed it until then. Or rather, until Helen had gone home. It was only then that it hit me, that I realised I couldn't live without her. Our farewell had been painful, to say the least. Anyhow, I called her two days after she'd left, and asked her to marry me.'

He broke off, was silent for so long that Elaine had to prompt him. 'Guy? You called her—and?'

'And she said yes, she felt exactly the same. I came over to England and stayed at her home, which was a hotel. Her parents ran a small hotel which they've now sold. They've retired. Helen and I married; I kept my house on in Florida, thinking it would be nice to spend winters there, which we did. But for the most part we lived in Cornwall. I loved Cornwall, still do, so I bought a house there and—and that's about it.'

Elaine forced herself to smile. 'That's hardly the end of

the story, Guy. Did Helen work?'

'Not after we married. She used to work for her parents in the hotel. She'd read literature and history at university, but she wasn't ambitious, not in the least. She was a bookworm, spent a lot of time reading, she also adored cooking, riding, sailing and—and life was good for us,' he finished dully.

'Jamie's only four. You—well, obviously you decided to wait before starting a family.'

'Actually, no. We were trying from the beginning, it just didn't happen. We'd been married seven years before she discovered she was pregnant. She—she died when Jamie was five months old.' His expression changed suddenly. Elaine saw the pain in his eyes and had to look away. His pain was her pain.

'I'm sorry, Guy. Very sorry. How—what happened?'

'It was an accident.' Even now, four years after the event, his voice was incredulous. 'A fluke. One of those crazy, unbelievable—she fell down a flight of stairs.'

'Dear Lord . . .'

'Remember the 'flu epidemic four winters ago? Helen's parents were quite ill with it. The hotel was closed for the winter. It was November—we didn't go to Florida that year because Jamie was just a tiny baby. He stayed at home with me when Helen went to stay with her parents for a few days, to look after them. On one of her journeys down to the kitchens she tripped on the stairs. She fell from top to bottom and knocked herself out. She never regained consciousness, Elaine. She was in hospital for nine days but . . . she died. Just died without ever regaining consciousness.'

'Guy! Oh, Guy——' She wanted desperately to go to him, put her arms around him, but something stopped her, something about him told her not to.

'So you see,' he said quietly, 'that day I met you, when I told you I understood how you were feeling, it was true. I knew what kind of shock you'd been through. It takes a long time to get over. I think you've coped admirably, Elaine, the way you've got things sorted out.'

'It was different for me. I lost my parents, you lost your *wife*, the mother of your child! It is different.'

'I suppose . . . hell, it's four years since Helen died and I still haven't sorted myself out.' With a wry smile he added, 'I'm being urged to remarry.'

'Urged by whom?'

'Virtually everyone. My family—I keep in touch with them. I have two brothers and a sister, all married, all with children. I don't go out of my way to cultivate friends, but I have a couple, good friends, in Cornwall, and they keep telling me to find a wife. Even my father-in-law recently asked me whether I'd thought about it. Of course I've relied so much on my in-laws, and it isn't fair to them, I know it. They live about half an hour's drive from my house in Cornwall. I mentioned they're retired now, they sold the hotel? When I'm at home they have Jamie for three, four days a week so I can work uninterrupted, which is why I go back at weekends from here, to take him to my house and give them a break.'

'It's heck of a drive to Cornwall, Guy.'

'That's no problem. To an American it isn't a long drive. All things are relative. One of my brothers lives on a farm out in the sticks now, near Kansas—and I mean in the sticks! He'd think nothing of driving several hundred miles to go to a party. I suppose——' He broke off, sighing. 'To get back to the point. My in-laws. Oh, they adore Jamie, there's no doubt about it, but looking after a four-year-old is hardly what they had planned for their retirement. They worked damned hard all their lives, I know it's their ambition to go on a world cruise, has been for years. I'll have to do something—I must sort myself out by next year.'

'Next year?'

'When Jamie's five. He'll be starting school. I can't keep shifting him from one house to another. And I've got to make up my mind whether to stay in England or go back to Florida, I still have my house there. Hell, maybe I should marry again. I don't know that I want it, but it would solve a lot of problems.'

Elaine's eyes closed briefly. Dear God, he was hardly thinking of marriage with the right motive, but—but she couldn't prevent herself from thinking what it would be like to be married to him . . . She forced herself to say something sensible; he was expecting a response. 'There is an alternative, as I mentioned earlier,' she said. 'Get yourself a housekeeper—a good one, living in. I'm surprised you haven't done it before now.'

'I've thought about it, obviously. I'm not sure I like the idea of someone living in. Now a wife would be——' A smile, the first real smile she'd seen today, brought back the light to his eyes. 'You wouldn't fancy the role, by any chance?'

It was difficult, very, to respond casually to that question. 'As what? Wife or housekeeper?'

'Either.'

Elaine looked away, trying desperately to think of something, anything, to change the subject entirely. He was joking, of course, but it hurt. He had no idea how much it hurt. 'The boxes! I'd forgotten about them. Why don't you make us a cup of coffee, then we can look through them.'

'I see. You know, that wasn't the subtlest change of subject I've ever witnessed!' His smile broadened. '*You* look through them. Their contents might be——'

'Full of dark secrets? Come on, show me where they are!' It was unfortunate she should choose that moment to go hunting through the things Guy had found in the loft, because her mood was low to begin with. But it really didn't occur to her that what she would find in the boxes would upset her further. She simply didn't think. At that moment all she wanted to do was get away from the thoughts going through her mind.

They were in a wardrobe in Guy's room. He took out the smallest first. 'This one's hefty. I'll stick it here.' He put it on the bed and Elaine sat next to it, tackling the string around it. She stopped, intrigued by the much bigger box he was dragging out.

'This one's as light as a feather, and this, a dead weight.'

'Oh, the intrigue! I'll start with the biggest! Have you got a knife or something?'

He was back in a moment with a pair of scissors, but Elaine had already dragged the string off the big box and opened it. It contained her mother's wedding dress, sealed in a plastic bag, old and dated but not in the least musty. Guy watched her as she opened the bag and held up the garment with its yards and yards of lace and net. The headdress was there, too, and a pair of white satin shoes.

'Elaine?'

'It's all right. I'm——' In truth, she was on the verge of tears. It had been quite the wrong time to do this, quite the wrong time.

'I'll go and get that coffee.'

When Guy came back she was sorting through the second box on the floor. Tears were no longer a threat. The contents of this box were very uninteresting. 'Old accounts and files on the business, going back yonks.' She took the coffee he handed her. 'Do you think I ought to keep them? They go back to my grandfather's day.'

'No. One isn't required to keep accounts going back that far! They're of no interest to you? I suppose you could ask Don whether he'd like to take a look at them.'

'There's no point. Had they been of any importance, Dad would have kept them locked away in the office.'

The box Guy had dumped on the bed, the last one, did make her cry. At any other time it probably wouldn't have, but all that Guy had told her, his speaking about his marriage to the woman he'd been so in love with, had made her susceptible, made her feel very vulnerable.

'My school books . . . I don't believe it!' There was more. The box contained exercise books, text books covering years of her earlier education. Even her first pencil box was there, and the first thing she'd ever made in her sewing class—a handkerchief case. 'My mother—but she wasn't a hoarder, fancy her keeping all this stuff. She . . .' The tears were sliding down her cheeks, and Guy's arms came around her.

It was exactly what she needed; he had taken hold of her before she had a chance to ask him to. 'Hold me tightly,' she murmured against him. 'Tightly, please!'

She leaned against him, taking strength from his strength, and it helped enormously. She didn't cry hard, the tears receded and in a moment or two she was reasonably composed. His arms were closed around her as they sat, and she moved, letting him know she was all right now. 'I'm sorry, it was just——'

'I know. I understand.'

'Oh, Guy, you're so——' Elaine didn't pause to think. She kissed him, unable to hold back, unable not to give vent somehow to all the emotions churning inside her.

That first kiss led rapidly to more. Within seconds Guy lay back on the bed, still holding her, pulling her against his entire length, moulding her body against his. The onslaught to Elaine's senses came thick and fast. There was the scent of him, from him and from the bed he slept in, there was the touch of his mouth against hers, lightly to begin with and then more and more demanding, a demand she was equal to. Then it was she who was demanding, arching hungrily against him as his hands began to explore her and she in turn touched him in

wonder at the size, the solid muscularity of him. Her
hands were beneath his shirt, revelling in the feel of him,
the smooth skin of his back, the movement of muscles,
the low moan her touch evoked.

'Elaine! God, I want you so much!' His lips were at her
throat, his hands parting the blouse she didn't even
realise he had unbuttoned. Then his hands were on her
breasts, inflaming her further until she too was softly
moaning. When his lips took over, covering the taut peak
of a nipple, her moan became a cry, a short, clear sound
which was almost a protest against the sheer, sensual
pleasure of it.

'Guy . . .' She heard another sound, something distant
but getting louder. It was a siren, the siren of an
ambulance or police car? She had no way of knowing. It
passed, faded rapidly, but it impinged just enough to
make her realise how far things had gone. She was on the
verge of making love with Guy. Here, of all places! On
her parents' bed. In broad daylight. 'Guy, let go of me,
please!' she said urgently.

'Elaine——'

'*Please*. I don't—this is all wrong. I feel——' She
pulled away, keeping her back to him as she rapidly
buttoned her blouse. How could she tell him how wrong it
felt? This room, this bed of all beds. It surely wouldn't
make sense to him. 'I—Guy, I'm sorry but——'

'Sorry!' He caught hold of her shoulder, twisting her
round to face him, his grey eyes darkened and cold with
anger. 'For the record, it wasn't I who started this little
scenario!'

'I know, I—didn't realise things would——' She
couldn't finish the sentence. Would happen so fast? Was
that what she was trying to say? Partly.

Guy pulled himself into a sitting position, swinging his
legs to the floor, his head dropping into his hands as he
ran his fingers through his hair. 'Get out of here, will

you? Go down and make some fresh coffee or something. Just—how the hell can you do this to me? What the hell do you think I'm made of?' Elaine got to the door before answering that, embarrassed, loving him, hating his anger with her, anxious. As she opened the door she turned, looking at him uncertainly. 'Sugar and spice?' she asked.

It worked. He threw a pillow at her.

She walked down to the kitchen quickly, chewing at her lower lip, well aware she had better not let anything like this happen again. She had tried his patience and found its limit. After all, she had instigated it. Next time she had better be prepared to finish what she started. Next time?

Inevitably there would be a next time.

She leaned against the sink, in need of support. What the devil was she going to do about this man? Have an affair with him, why not? There were plenty of reasons why not, not least the fact that he would only be around a few more months. How would she feel then? Even worse than she felt now! Although there was something to be said—

'Elaine?' The sound of his voice shocked her. She spun around. 'I—didn't hear you come down.'

His anger had gone, but he wasn't exactly looking pleased with her. 'I want you to do something.'

She was biting her lip again, wondering what was going through his mind. 'Yes?'

'I want you to think about my proposal. When I asked you earlier if you fancied the job—as housekeeper or wife, I wasn't wholly serious, as you know. But think about it. You once told me the most important ingredient for marriage, in your view, is compatibility. So think about us, you and me, separately and together. Compatibility is something we do have. Think about your life-style and about mine. It could work, could work very well indeed.'

She was staring at him. He was proposing—*marriage*? So calmly, so coolly? 'You can't be serious!' she protested.

'Oh, I'm serious all right. Absolutely. No, don't say anything now. Think about it.'

'But——'

'Think about it!'

'Guy, you can't just——'

'I said think about it, that's all I'm asking of you. When you've thought it over we'll discuss it again. Let me know in your own good time. End of conversation for now. Switch that kettle off, we're going out. Come on, I need some fresh air.'

Guy spent the following week-end in Cornwall. He didn't want to bring Jamie north again so soon, for two reasons: firstly, it would involve twice the amount of driving and he could ill afford the time. Secondly, he thought it a good idea to leave Elaine to herself for a few days, he said, to think over his proposal without the influence of his presence.

She didn't need to think it over. She wanted to say yes. Yes, yes, yes! But that wasn't what she was going to say. She was going to refuse.

Had she seen Guy the following week, she might have told him no. But she didn't see him. When he hadn't phoned her by Wednesday, she phoned him, getting frantic in case he had had an accident.

He was there. 'Guy! You're home! I was worried——'

'Hey, I'm sorry. Didn't know you cared!' It was a throwaway line, one of those things people say. But he probably believed it, more or less. He had no idea of the extent of her feelings for him. 'It was thoughtless of me not to call you,' he went on. 'But I did get back only last night, very late. I had to spend a day in London, to see my agent. I've been working solidly since I got in, needless to say. I'll have to stay with it, Elaine, so give me a few more days. The book's not going as well as I'd expected. Too many other things on my mind, I suppose . . .' He waited for a response. She didn't make one.

She was grateful he couldn't see her. Her eyes were bright with unshed tears. It was, really, a ridiculous situation. In other circumstances she would have read this as a brush-off. As things were, he had asked her to marry him, for heaven's sake. Those other things on his mind—she was one of them. She, and his problems, one of which *was* her. If past experience was anything to go by, he would keep his distance physically as if she had the plague. He wouldn't lay a finger on her.

God, what a mess, a ridiculous mess! Yet there was no way she would agree to marry him; he didn't love her. *Love* her? Did he need to? What about her theories, the ones she had had before she was sure how she felt about him? They still held, didn't they? He didn't need to love her to make a success of marriage to her.

She had been through all this a hundred times since she'd last seen him, and she had reached no conclusions. There were no answers. It was all hypothetical.

'. . . Are you still there, Elaine? I said which do you want first, the bad news or the very bad news?'

''Course I'm here.' She put a smile in her voice. 'Fire away. I'll have the bad news first.'

'They've re-scheduled the filming on *Another Time.*'

'What?'

'*Another Time, Another*——'

'Yes, yes, I know the title. What filming? You've never mentioned this.'

'Haven't I? Well, they're making a television series of it, they were supposed to start filming—I mean the part on location in Cornwall—next February. It's been rescheduled to start in early January. And I'll have to be there. I'm sorry I haven't mentioned it; to be honest, I'd filed it away in my mind and forgotten about it. I worked on the film script ages ago—or what seems like ages ago. Anyway, you see the implications?'

'Not really . . .'

'I'm getting crowded, it means I'll have to buckle down and finish what I'm doing. There's no way I want to leave this book unfinished, then start again after the filming. My mind doesn't work like that. All of which is fine, all of which I can cope with. But then there's the very bad news.'

Elaine had been standing by the phone. She sat, now, her heart heavy, worrying. 'Go on.'

'Jamie's grandmother has to go in to hospital for minor surgery on her foot. She'll be in hospital for just a few days, but she won't be able to move around for two or three weeks. I'm going to have to bring Jamie up here; there's no way my father-in-law will be able to cope with both of them.'

'Oh, Guy, don't worry about that! Jamie can come to me. It's no problem. I'll have him.'

'Elaine, it's sweet of you but——'

'But it's what you hoped I'd say! Come on, Guy, we know each other better than that! Of course I'll have him, I'll be glad to. Honestly! I've got a fold-away bed.'

'You could move in here for a few weeks . . .'

'Forget *that*!'

He was laughing. 'I already have. I've just considered how much of a distraction you might prove to be!'

'Listen, seriously, do you think Jamie will be happy about this?' Elaine asked him.

'I'm sure he will.'

'You haven't mentioned it to him?'

'No, I have not. I had *not* taken you for granted, Elaine.'

No, she should have known he wouldn't do that. 'When's his grandmother going into hospital? And what's her name, by the way?'

'Esther. She's going in privately—so the answer is, as soon as I've sorted something out.'

'Then it's up to you. You can bring Jamie whenever you like. You've—you've told your in-laws about me, I take it?'

'Long since. Look, I'd better go, I've left the printer rattling away. I'll call you later in the week, make arrangements to see you.'

Elaine's house-guest came on the second weekend in October. It might have been more sensible for her and Guy to swap houses, but neither of them thought of it. As it was, with Jamie's clothes and things and the fold-away bed in the living room, her cottage was well and truly overcrowded. But they coped, she and Jamie.

He was a good child, really no trouble to her at all. She loved having him around. During the first week, he was with her every day in her work-room, 'helping' her, fascinated by what she was doing and trying to copy her. Early the following week his father came and took over for a day while Elaine went out to make some deliveries and see her customers.

When Jamie became a little restless during the third week, she wrapped him up well and let him play in the garden when he wanted to, or watch TV. She also took him out for drives, recognising his need for new stimulus, a change of scenery. 'When's Daddy coming to see us again?' he asked on the Wednesday.

'This evening, darling.'

'Before I go to bed?'

'Of course! You can't see him if you're asleep, can you?'

He hooted at that. 'You are funny, Elaine! Much more

than Gran. She doesn't do fun things with me, like you do.'

'Well, she's older, Jamie. She probably hasn't got as much energy as I have.'

'Gran's nice, though.'

'I'm sure she is.'

'But I don't think having a grandmother is the same as having a mother.' He turned to her, his face troubled. 'I never had a mother, so I don't know.'

Elaine brought the car to a halt, swallowing against the lump in her throat. Dear God, he was so like Guy, so beautiful . . . 'Everyone has a mother, darling. Unfortunately, they can't always stay with us.'

'Your mother went to God, too, didn't she? Daddy told me.'

Guy got to the cottage at five that evening. October had just slipped into November, the clocks had gone back and the days were growing much shorter. By the look of it, Guy's days were getting longer. She dreaded to think how many hours' work he was putting in right now; he looked exhausted. Elaine put a hand on his cheek, her fingers brushing lightly over the skin beneath his eyes. 'You look shattered, Guy, and I'll bet you haven't had a decent meal since you were last here.'

She and Jamie had been home for an hour and were preparing a meal. He had insisted on helping.

'Your son,' she went on, 'is becoming a dab hand at peeling potatoes.'

'Gran never lets me do it—she thinks I can't do it properly,' Jamie put in.

Which of course was quite right, he couldn't, but Elaine always praised him for his efforts, whatever he was attempting. What difference if she had to finish the job? She believed children should be given a lot of encouragement and praise. She didn't need to have a child of her own to realise it could only be a good thing.

'Anyhow, I was thinking,' Jamie went on, turning to look at Elaine. 'If you married Daddy it would be nice. We could all live together in the same house and you could be my mother. I'd like that.'

Elaine's eyes flew to his father's. Surely, surely he hadn't put this idea in the child's head? Not before they'd discussed things? The question was in her eyes.

Not a word, he told her silently. I promise you, I haven't said a word to him.

'Daddy? Why don't you say something?' urged Jamie. 'Isn't it a good idea? I think it is!'

Guy was clearly at a loss. Elaine came to the rescue. '*I've* had a good idea! How would you like to sleep in *my* bed tonight, Jamie?' She had to talk to Guy. Tonight. It couldn't wait any longer.

'I'd love to! Will you be in it?'

'That's up to you. Not if you don't want me to. I could sleep in your bed in the living room.'

'No, I'd like it . . . I think!'

Elaine had to bite her cheeks to prevent herself laughing. The expression on Guy's face was a classic. 'Let me know what you think of it, son,' he said to the child, his eyes not leaving hers for a second.

They put Jamie to bed together, two teddies and all. 'Are you sure there'll be room for me?' Elaine asked laughingly.

'Yes! You don't make a noise like Gran, do you? She snores, I've heard her.'

'I—Guy, what are you grinning about?'

'I'm just desperate to hear the answer! Well?'

'How should I know? I hope not!' She backed out of the room.

'Elaine!' Jamie sat bolt upright. 'Don't turn the light off. You know I don't sleep with no lights!'

'I'm sorry, darling, I meant to switch the lamp on. Guy?'

Guy switched the bedside lamp on. It was Jamie's habit to have a lamp on until he went to sleep. Every evening so far, Elaine had left one on in the living room and had gone upstairs to work until bed-time. It hadn't been the most convenient of arrangements.

When she and Guy were settled downstairs he told her he had spoken to Esther that afternoon. 'She's getting about quite well now. She suggested I take Jamie down on Sunday.'

Even the thought of that was a wrench. 'But——' Elaine stopped the protest. 'I've fallen in love with him, Guy. You knew that would happen, didn't you?'

'On the contrary. You might have felt shackled. I have to say I'm relieved to hear it. Can I take it you're about to give me your answer, Elaine? It has to be why you put Jamie in your bed tonight—lucky little devil.'

She couldn't joke around, not now. Nor did she beat about the bush. There was no point in going into whys and wherefores, it simply wasn't necessary. 'I'll marry you, Guy,' she said. 'It makes a lot of sense, for you, for me, for Jamie. You and I are compatible, that much is obvious. I can work anywhere, like you; I don't have to live here. And I'm fond of you.' The words came out unbelievably calmly—how, she would never know. 'I believe you're fond of me, too.'

He didn't move, didn't give any clue as to what was going through his mind. 'Fond of you?' he said quietly. 'Yes, I can safely say I'm fond of you.'

He didn't ask her whether she were sure about her decision, he didn't need to. He was aware she had given it a great deal of thought, though he would never know the full extent of it.

'When?' she asked. 'And where?'

'As soon as practicable. Here in the north. There are two reasons for that. Your friends are here, and— well . . .'

'That's okay. I'm a step ahead of you. It's sweet of you not to want to say it, so I'll say it. It wouldn't be the most tactful thing in the world to have your in-laws present.'

'Elaine, I'm not sure. I'll sound them out. If they want to be there——'

'Then of course they may. I don't mind either way, Guy. But—yes, I do think it would be a nice gesture—right—to introduce me to them first. Rather than just presenting me as your wife.'

'I agree. So come down to Cornwall with me on Sunday; we'll tell them the news then. As for the date—we'd better think about that. There's a lot to do, a hell of a lot to organise.'

They plunged into a long discussion. Elaine sealed off the part of her which was still protesting, still unsatisfied. Only once did it surface, in a moment of sudden panic. 'Guy—I could live with you. There's really no need for us to marry, is there?'

He looked shocked, actually shocked. But it wasn't for any moral reason. 'There's a child involved, remember? I don't think living together is a good idea at all. I don't want Jamie to hear talk of Daddy with his live-in girlfriend. And I don't think it would add to his sense of security, such as it is. Elaine, either you're prepared to make a commitment or you're not. We've got a lot going for us, if you'll just think——'

Think? Dear God, she had thought herself inside out! 'I'm prepared, Guy. It was just an idea. I—perhaps I just wanted to be sure you were sure. About marriage, I mean. You see, I—well, you know my views on it. But what I didn't tell you is that I take it very seriously. In my book marriage is for keeps.'

He looked directly at her, holding her gaze. 'In mine, too.' Then he looked away. 'But of course it doesn't always work out like that, does it?'

CHAPTER FIVE

ELAINE and Guy were married at St John's Church near Tottington on the morning of the first Saturday in December, just two days before her twenty-third birthday. She had wanted to marry in church and Guy had been happy with the idea, leaving all the arrangements and organisation to her. She had kept it simple, all of it, from the white silk dress and jacket she had bought to the reception, which was to be in Don Black's home. He had insisted on doing that for her.

It was a small congregation, but Elaine's friends were all there, plus the staff from Faraday & Faraday and, happily, her one surviving relative, her cousin Philip. He had driven up from London the previous afternoon and would stay at *Rosalie* that night, before going home on Sunday. Guy's in-laws were not present but Jamie was: he had wanted to be. He'd been driven up the previous day by Guy's friends and nearest neighbours in Cornwall, Paul and Anna Masters. Paul was driving Jamie back to Cornwall, too. It was only in this that Guy had interfered with Elaine's plans. She had naturally assumed Jamie would drive down with her or Guy, in her car or his. They were leaving straight after the reception. But Guy had said no, he had arranged that Jamie would go with Paul and Anna would drive Elaine's car home, because he and Elaine were taking a 'detour' en route to Cornwall. That was all she had been able to get out of him.

The ceremony went perfectly, but it was tinged by sadness on two counts. Elaine could have hoped for more, much more, as far as her new husband's feelings for her were concerned. There was that and . . . and the absence of the two people she so missed, the two people in the world who should have been at her wedding.

The bride and groom emerged into the pale December sunlight to find themselves confronted by a reporter and a press photographer whose camera was already clicking, taking both of them by surprise. Guy refused to make any comment whatsoever, ushering Elaine into the waiting car before their own photographer could snap more than a few hurried shots.

'Damn!' They both said the word. Elaine continued, 'I'm sorry, Guy, I can't imagine who told the press——'

'A neighbour, probably. Who knows? It doesn't matter. I'm sorry about *our* photographer, he can take some shots at the reception, okay?'

She nodded. 'That doesn't matter, either.'

Guy sensed her sadness. He knew she was thinking about her parents; he held her hand tightly in his on the drive from the church to Don's house. He didn't say anything, nor did he need to, his support and understanding were enough for her. She leaned her head on his shoulder, relieved the ceremony was over. Relieved and nervous and, yes, a little afraid of the future.

There had been so very much to do, to organise, for her and her husband. *Rosalie* was up for sale yet again. Well, it was good business for the solicitors! Don had been marvellous: he was going to handle the sale of *Rosalie* for Guy, lock stock and barrel, with luck, as he had bought the house. If that couldn't be achieved, he was going to dispose of the contents anyway. Elaine had thought a dozen times how crazy life could be, the way things had turned out. Here she was, married to the man she had sold her parents' house to, becoming a wife and a mother within the space of five months. How far away last July seemed, that sunny day when Guy had walked into her office, demanding to see the boss.

At least they didn't have to worry about selling Elaine's cottage—it was rented. The entire contents, every last stick, together with Guy's word processor and printer, had been packed and despatched by road to Cornwall only the previous morning, to be met at Guy's house by his father-in-law. There was plenty of room for Elaine's belongings in Guy's house, the size of which had come as a shock to her, and she had every intention of setting up a work-room in it. Plenty of tourists visited Cornwall—there would be no shortage of gift shops to sell her wares to.

The past few weeks had been hectic, chaotic, to say the least, culminating in a semblance of order, just about, the previous afternoon when Jamie had arrived with Paul and Anna, and Philip had arrived safely an hour later. They had all slept at *Rosalie*, Jamie in Guy's bed, Elaine in her own, old single bed, Paul and Anna in the guest bed downstairs, Philip on a settee. Elaine wouldn't hear of their booking into hotels. They would manage, she had said. And they had.

Since the weekend he had taken her down to Cornwall, following her agreement to marry him, she had seen hardly anything of Guy. He had been working to his maximum in an effort to complete the draft of his book, which he had. He would have the finished typescript ready, he said, by Christmas.

'Elaine?' They were outside Don's house. 'Are you falling asleep on me? What sort of bride are you?'

She smiled, responding to his teasing, hiding any trace of the worry flitting through her mind. It was a good question: what sort of bride was she? She shook herself. Come on, Elaine, you've made your bed . . . She groaned inwardly; there was her answer: nervous. She was a nervous bride. Well, that was normal enough, wasn't it? If only everything else were normal about this wedding.

Stop it, she told herself. Whatever else may be lacking

between you and Guy, at least you're good friends. So relax, everything's going to be all right.

Congratulations and good wishes, guests taking photographs. Champagne, chatter, food she had to force herself to nibble at. More photographs, laughter and teasing. The reception was normal enough, too, there were no hitches, no sign of the press when she and Guy left to change their clothes, pick up their remaining bits and pieces from *Rosalie*.

They closed the front door of the house, finally, with a sigh of relief, climbed into Guy's Porsche and headed south. It was minutes before either of them spoke.

'I've never heard of two newlyweds being so exhausted within hours of getting married!' laughed Elaine.

Guy glanced at her, raising an eyebrow. 'Are you trying to tell me something, Mrs Harris? If so, I've suddenly gone deaf.'

Mrs Harris. *Mrs Guy Harris.*

She couldn't laugh at what he'd just said. He must have caught her change of expression, because his hand reached over to touch hers reassuringly. 'Don't worry, we're going to get away from it all for a couple of days. Relax a little.'

'Where are we going?' she asked him.

'That's my secret—and mine alone. Somewhere cosy and warm and luxurious. To a hotel, of course. I think we deserve to be waited on hand and foot, don't you? I'm only sorry we can't manage a couple of weeks, but that would have been impossible.'

'Of course.' She hadn't expected a honeymoon of any duration.

'I'll make it up to you, Elaine, next year,' Guy promised. 'For starters we'll take a vacation in Florida as soon as we can. I'd like you to see the place, see whether you might like to settle there. Much as I adore Cornwall, I can't say the British winters do much for me!'

She looked at him, loving him so much it hurt. And . . . well, he was fond of her, there was that much.

How different this must be from his first wedding day, his marriage to the wife he had been madly in love with. Helen. Elaine turned to look out of the window, not wanting Guy to realise the full extent of her anxiety. She was thinking not only about Helen but also about Helen's parents.

Her father, Edward Richardson, had been charming to Elaine on meeting her the previous month. He had fussed over her and had done his utmost to make her feel welcome in his house. To be fair, so had Esther Richardson. But she hadn't succeeded. Elaine had sensed her underlying resentment, understandable though it was, carefully covered though it was. Not carefully enough, however. In talking to Elaine she had mentioned her daughter several times. 'Do you enjoy cooking, Elaine? Helen did, she was a wonderful cook!'

There had been remarks such as that, not intended to hurt but hurting just the same. There had been one very difficult moment, when Esther's eyes had grown moist, when she had said to Guy, 'Yesterday was the anniversary of Helen's death. Four years. I trust you remembered that, Guy?'

Esther might be a problem. Oh, she had been friendly enough, but—Elaine was not Helen. She was not Jamie's mother. Nor was Guy even in love with her—nobody pretended that was the case. It was understood by everyone that she and Guy were . . . good friends who had decided to marry because it made a lot of sense for all concerned.

She could hear in her head her own words, spoken more than once. 'Yes, well, life wasn't the same for me after my family died. I felt lonely, living in that cottage by myself. Guy's been a great comfort to me in many ways.'

She had said something very similar to Paul and Anna Masters, whom she had liked instantly on being introduced to. Anna had given her a very searching look but had made no comment. Elaine, Guy and Jamie had spent an afternoon with them and their child. Theirs was the nearest house to Guy's—about half a mile away, inland.

Guy's house couldn't be any closer to the sea and had been not at all what Elaine had expected, not that she had actually conjured up a picture of the place. Apart from thinking of it as once having been Helen's home, she hadn't speculated about it at all. It was a few miles south of Penzance, perched on a cliff-side down which there was a path leading to a sandy patch of beach, a little cove which was private and went with the house.

The house stood in three acres of grounds skirted by woods which added even more to its privacy. Elaine had loved that, loved the ruggedness of the grounds and the surroundings of Guy's home. Close to the house there were flower beds she couldn't wait to get her hands on, to the rear a big lawn broken by bushes and mature shrubs. From the outside the house itself looked like a large version of a log cabin, its façade predominantly wood. The rooms were airy, spacious, all with vast picture windows and gorgeous views. The ground floor was split-level, the kitchen to the rear, the living room overlooking the sea. There were four bedrooms en suite on the first floor, Guy's study being on the second floor. There were two more rooms up there, too, large rooms. Both empty. For the moment.

Guy had bought the place from its architect. 'He'd lived in it since he had it built nineteen years ago,' he'd told her. 'I couldn't believe my luck when I found it. I can't imagine why he wanted to leave. I didn't ask!'

They were leaving the motorway now. Elaine stretched as best she could in the confines of the car. 'Can we stop somewhere for a cup of coffee, Guy?' she asked. 'I'm parched!'

'Sure. We're still about an hour away from our hotel.'

Their hotel was south of Banbury, a secluded country house standing alone in acres of beautifully-tended grounds which began with a long sweeping driveway off a country lane. The interior was welcoming, managing somehow to be both smart and homely at the same time. Elaine returned the receptionist's smile as Guy signed the register: Mr and Mrs G. Harris.

A young porter showed them upstairs to their room, which turned out to be a suite, complete with sitting room and bathroom. Elaine was delighted. 'Oh, Guy, this is lovely, how clever of you to find this place!'

The sitting-room was more like a boudoir, except there was a TV in it. On a circular table stood a silver bowl full of roses which must have cost a fortune at that time of year. At the side of it, already on ice in a bucket, was a bottle of vintage champagne. Elaine blinked at that. 'How did——'

Her husband was smiling at her. 'It's all done with telephones.'

'Do they know you here? You—haven't been here before, by any chance?' She couldn't prevent herself from asking, she wanted to dispel intrusive thoughts that Guy might have been here with Helen . . . maybe in this same suite.

'Never set eyes on the place till today. Someone once mentioned it to me saying how pleasant it was, and I happened to remember its name.'

'The flowers, you organised those, too.' White roses, as had been the flowers he'd given her that first evening they had spent together. 'It was thoughtful of you, I appreciate it.'

'The ones in the bedroom are on the house,' he grinned.

The bedroom. Elaine hadn't looked in there yet. Guy had gone in when the porter brought them up. 'I'd better go in there and unpack.' She wanted to hang the dress she would wear at dinner: it was of the sort of material that didn't take kindly to being folded for long.

'I'll give you five minutes. Don't want this champagne to get too cold.'

Elaine made her escape, grateful for a few minutes alone. It was all so perfect here, but . . . She stopped short at the sight of the bed dominating the room. It wasn't merely king-sized, it was seven feet square, set back into an arched recess above which was a semi-circular canopy draped in the same pink silk of the coverlet. The theme of this room was pink, pale, chalky pinks of various shades except for the carpet and furniture, which was white. She opened a door to take a peep in the en suite bathroom. The colours of the bedroom were repeated in here, its blinds, towels, tiles and carpeting all blending. The bath itself was the sort that fitted in a corner—and was big enough for two. She stood looking at it, her imagination running riot.

Back in the bedroom she stepped out of her shoes, glancing once more at the huge bed, her imagination working overtime again, bringing with it an undeniable rush of excitement. She opened her case, not knowing whether she should unpack Guy's case, too. Would he expect her to? She was about to call to him and ask, but the words never formed themselves. In her case, on top of the clothes she had packed so carefully that morning, were several layers of something made from heavy, ivory-coloured satin. It was not gift-wrapped, but there was a card tucked among the folds. Anna Masters! 'Please forgive the liberty I've taken,' it said, 'but I thought you should have something very beautiful to wear tonight.'

Both smiling and despondent, Elaine held up the full-length satin negligee and a matching nightdress with skimpy straps and an almost non-existent bodice. 'Oh, Anna!' she whispered. She couldn't wear this—she might as well not wear anything. It was too much, too little! She'd feel like a vamp.

Her own nightdress and housecoat, her best, the ones she had laundered and pressed meticulously, were— missing! '*Anna!* I'll never forgive you for this!'

'What did you say?' called Guy.

'I—nothing,' she called back. 'I mean, I was wondering whether I should unpack your things?'

'Heck, leave that. Come and relax, have a cigarette and a glass of champagne.'

Guy was already relaxed. Perfectly. He was lying on a chaise-longue in the sitting room, his jacket, shoes and tie discarded, the top buttons of his shirt undone. He got up the instant Elaine joined him. 'What's the matter, has something displeased you?'

'Not at all! It's—what a lovely idea, having a real fire in here!' It wasn't needed, the hotel was centrally heated, but it was nice.

Small talk. In her nervousness she had been reduced to that. Guy didn't seem to notice. They drank some champagne and she talked about the hotel, their wedding, the reception, the drive down here. Anything.

'Well, I think I'll take a bath before dinner,' Guy said at length. 'It's turned six. I've arranged to have our meal served in here, I hope that's okay with you?'

'Lovely. What luxury!' What could she say? He had gone to so much trouble.

'Do you want the bathroom first?' Guy asked her.

'No. I—after you.'

He disappeared into the bedroom, not bothering to close the door. He turned the radio on and Elaine tried to concentrate on the music. She couldn't. She was thinking about the negligee set: she had never owned anything so frivolous; it wasn't her image, that sort of thing. Could she pluck up the courage to wear it?

Guy left her with no choice. He came back into the sitting room wearing a towelling dressing gown ... and probably nothing else—even his feet were bare. 'Bathroom's free.'

'Aren't you going to get dressed?'

'Why should we bother?' He sprawled in an armchair, shrugging. 'We're eating up here.'

Elaine concentrated on her glass, draining the last drop before getting up. She swayed slightly: she had had no breakfast, very little to eat at the reception, and the champagne had gone to her head. She didn't mind in the least, it was helping to loosen the knot of tension inside her, helping her see the funny side of her dilemma. By the time she got in the bath she was giggling.

She was doing it again when she finally faced Guy. He heard her moving around in the bedroom. 'Ah, you're out at last! It's just as well—I called room service a minute ago and told them to send up our dinner.'

Elaine stood in the doorway of the room, giggling and blushing her way through an explanation about her nightwear.

Guy couldn't take his eyes off her. 'I don't care whether it's your style or not, I think it's delicious!'

Dinner was delicious, too. It was wheeled in by a smiling, immaculately clad waiter who whisked a white linen cloth from the trolley and draped it across the table in the corner. Within seconds everything was ready for them.

The meal was something else Guy had organised prior to their arrival. Every dish was a favourite of Elaine's: the smoked salmon, the chicken breasts cooked in a white wine sauce, the light, fluffy chocolate mousse to finish. And there was more champagne.

She called a halt after two more glasses, though the

food had helped counteract its effects. 'You're not trying to get me drunk, are you?' she laughed.

'Absolutely not.' Guy looked at her, his grey eyes showing no sign of amusement. 'I'm trying to get you to relax, that's all.' He reached across the table, put his hand over hers. 'You're tense and nervous, and there's no need for it, you know.'

'Guy——'

'No, you don't need to explain anything. Don't reason, don't rationalise. Just finish your meal and be comfortable with me.'

Be comfortable with me. She smiled at him, relaxing visibly. 'Thank you for this dinner. All my favourite dishes—I've so enjoyed it.'

When they had finished eating, Guy excused himself. 'Back in a moment. There's something I almost forgot . . .' He came back with a tiny, velvet-covered box, saying nothing as he placed it on the table in front of her.

Elaine opened it tentatively, gasping when she saw the beautiful diamond solitaire nestling inside. 'Guy! I can't—you can't——'

'I can, you will. It's your engagement ring. After all, we *were* engaged—we just didn't have time to go out and buy a ring!'

'It's so beautiful!' She slipped it on her wedding finger. A perfect fit. 'How did you know? You weren't with me when I chose my wedding ring.'

'No, but they knew your size in the shop, didn't they? So that's something else I've learned about you.'

It was after the waiter had returned, to bring coffee and remove everything else, that Guy picked up on that conversation. 'There's still a lot I don't know about you, though.'

'There is? Like what?'

'Like whether you can dance.'

"*Dance?* Of course I can! I might have been living like

a hermit these past few years, but I did have a youth, one I enjoyed very much.'

He laughed at that. 'You still are. That's what I mean, I mean can you dance in the *old-fashioned* way?'

Elaine got to her feet, pushed back the armchair she'd been sitting on. 'I like a challenge. Okay, Buster, I can see you don't believe me. On your feet!' She didn't stop to think what she was doing, that she was by no means drunk but she was certainly tipsy; all she knew was that suddenly she felt like dancing, now he had mentioned it. The music drifting in from the bedroom was perfect for it. 'I take it *you* can dance?'

'After a fashion.'

His 'fashion' proved almost too much for her. He was good, very good. He took hold of her in an almost businesslike manner, firmly but not too close, and led her into steps she hadn't used in years. 'Elaine! I thought you said you could dance!' he teased.

'Hey, give me a minute! I'm rusty. And you said you danced *after a fashion*——'

'I do! A damned good one!'

She burst out laughing. Guy was having none of it. 'Stop that. Don't fidget, dance. Show me what you can do.'

She did. For several minutes she coped extremely well and was enjoying herself enormously. Then another thought struck her and this time she couldn't stop laughing. 'I've just realised, what on earth must we look like, you dancing in your dressing gown and me in this thing?'

'Happy. If anyone could see us, they'd think we looked happy.'

Elaine sobered at that. 'And are you? Are you happy, Guy?'

He stopped dancing, holding her closer now, his hand reaching to stroke her hair, his eyes looking deeply into hers. 'Yes,' he whispered. 'Yes, my lovely girl, I am.'

Closing what space was left between them, she slid her arms around his neck, all remaining nervousness vanishing completely as his mouth claimed hers. She wanted him. Now. Just as much as he wanted her. A moment later he lifted her into his arms and carried her to the bed.

But Guy was in no hurry, no hurry at all. He turned the radio down so it was only just audible, switched one bedside lamp on before kissing her again. And again. He kissed her into a frenzy; her arousal had been immediate, but he took his time with her, stroking her, his hands exploring her body until she had no sense of time or place or anything, anything but him and her need of him. 'Guy, please, take me now. Make love to me, please!'

'Sssh.' He kissed the tip of her nose. 'That's precisely what I intend to do.' His lips moved to her temple, her closed eyelids, before descending once more to her mouth. With his mouth he made love to her, moving erotically in an appetiser of what was to come.

'Guy, Guy, please!' Her negligee had long been discarded, now he took off her nightdress, his eyes moving over her naked body for the first time.

'My God, you're so beautiful . . .' He was caressing her again, touching confidently but gently that most intimate part of her.

Elaine cried out against the pleasure of it, a protest against an excitement she felt she could no longer tolerate. It still didn't get her what she wanted. She reached for him, letting instinct be her tutor, thrilling with a new delight at the groan her actions drew from him.

A few moments later they were joined, as one, and the wonder began all over again, the kissing, the caressing. Now Guy was inside her, now she knew what it was to be made love to. Had she been capable of thinking at all, she might have asked herself how she had lived for so long without such pleasure.

Guy was still very much in control, though she hadn't the experience to realise it, making love to her slowly, gently, until in time she was thrusting against him with a new hunger, a hunger which became a frantic need, a swelling and mounting of desire, the final, ultimate satisfaction of which had her crying out. Guy's name. Over and over again.

Elaine clung to him, her face against his neck, smiling. They were still joined, both perfectly still now, Guy holding her tightly as he felt the relaxation seeping through her body.

'Darling Elaine . . .' Very, very lightly he kissed her mouth, waiting before moving his body with infinite slowness, waiting until hers responded in encouragement.

She closed her eyes as his kiss deepened. It was starting all over again . . .

Hours later, wrapped in Guy's arms, she woke. The radio was still playing softly, the lamp was still on. She didn't move. She looked at her husband and smiled serenely at the memory of their lovemaking. Seconds later Guy opened his eyes. She kissed him, as he had kissed her face earlier, his mouth, his cheeks, his temples, and within minutes it was starting all over again . . .

CHAPTER SIX

ELAINE didn't mind. How could she mind?

They were on the motorway, heading for Cornwall. Heading for home. It was Monday morning, a freezing, rainy December morning. Until a couple of hours ago, when they had gone down for breakfast in the dining room of their hotel, she and Guy had not set foot outside their rooms.

Now, with the cold light of day there had been the realisation that on Saturday, from the moment they'd walked into their hotel, her husband had been seducing her. She smiled inwardly. How could she possibly mind that? She didn't, of course she didn't. But it was important not to allow any illusions to start forming. Even in the throes of passion, that wonderful, wondrous passion they had shared, Guy had not uttered one endearment, one word that he would not have said to her at any other time. So it had been an honest seduction. It had been planned, engineered, but only with the intention of pleasing her, helping her to relax, to shed her nervousness, so that she could drift, would drift, spontaneously into making love with him.

The difference between them and any other newly married couple was that his planning had been necessary. He had not taken her for granted in any way, nor should he have, yet given that they were married, that in itself was wrong. In other words they did not have love to fall back on, love as a binding agent, love, which would make actions and reactions automatic, his planning and her tension unnecessary. Her love for him was unspoken and would remain that way. His for her was merely a hope that lay in the future. Maybe he would learn to love her, in time. Right now it did not exist. He had made love to her, would make love to her again, not as an expression of love but of a physical need, plain and simple.

Which was fine, all of it. After all, she had walked into this situation, this marriage, knowing the score detail by detail. She was merely taking stock, that was all. It had been a marvellous weekend, regardless of anything, but it could surely do no harm just to remind herself exactly what was what. Especially now, now that the honeymoon was over.

Some organisation was on the agenda now. In talking to Anna the previous month Elaine had learned that her child, a little girl a few months younger than Jamie, went to play school three mornings a week. Elaine was going to enrol Jamie after Christmas—she had already sounded him out and had been met with enthusiasm. In mentioning it to Guy he had agreed wholeheartedly with her, had explained that because Jamie was with his grandparents most of the time, his going to play school had been impractical. Edward Richardson drove a car, but it would have been too much to expect him to take the child to and fro for part-time sessions three days a week. 'They do more than enough for me already,' Guy had said. Well, Elaine would take Jamie.

There was the house to sort out, too. She turned to him, thinking about that. 'Guy, I told you I'd like my work-room to be the one that overlooks the back of your house, didn't I?' She could keep an eye on Jamie from there, when he was playing on his swing in the back garden. She could also look out over the woods.

'Our house, Elaine. It's our house now. Yes. You haven't changed your mind, have you?'

She glanced at him again. His last words came out strangely. 'No, I was just going to add that I plan on putting the furniture from the cottage, or most of it, in the room next door. I'm going to make it into another sitting-room. Is that okay?'

'You don't have to ask. You are the mistress of the house now. You do with it as you please.'

'The mistress of the house.' She mulled the words over. 'Mm. I think I like the sound of that.'

'What? Being a mistress?' He grinned, his hand sneaking over and slipping between her thighs.

Elaine promptly put it back on the steering wheel. 'Guy, I'm trying to plan ahead!'

'That's what I was doing.' He was still grinning. 'Just a little into the future—like what I'm going to do to you when I get you home.'

It wasn't easy not to laugh. '*I'm* doing some serious planning. I was——' She broke off, seeing the fleeting frown cross his face. 'What's the matter?'

'I was just thinking about my in-laws. Are they still my in-laws, now I've married you? Or are they "ex"?'

'I don't know! Anyhow, what about them?'

'Old Edward is enchanted by you,' Guy told her. 'I'm not so sure about Esther.'

'It's understandable.'

'But is it? Is it? Elaine, Helen is dead. *I've* come to terms with that.'

'I know, Guy, but her mother sees me as an interloper whether it makes sense or not. *And* I'm about to take over her only grandchild. Don't worry about it; I'm an unknown quantity to her at present. She'll be fine with me once she gets to know me. I'm not at all worried about it. You're thinking about Christmas, aren't you?'

'Yes. It would have been very difficult to refuse, since we're going to be in Cornwall anyway.'

They—no, Elaine—had been consulted about Christmas, had accepted Esther's invitation to spend the day with them. She was fully aware that Esther had done it for two reasons. Firstly, it was a thermometer: had

Elaine refused, it might have been taken as a slight, an act of unfriendliness, a signal that she was going to take over like a new broom. Secondly, simply, Esther wanted to see her grandson, if not as much as she saw him now, then at least regularly and especially at Christmas. 'It never occurred to me to refuse,' she told Guy firmly. 'I'm not going to keep Jamie away from his gran because she's your first wife's mother, which is probably what she's afraid of.'

She did not, of course, go on to say it, but she thought the situation must be as difficult for Guy as it was for Esther. Every time he saw Esther he would inevitably think of Helen. And it must be painful.

As for Elaine—well, she *was* an interloper, she *felt* like one, but she wasn't going to let anyone else know it. If things were going to work naturally and normally, she had to behave like a wife, like one who belonged, like the mistress of the house.

They got to the house at dusk. Her new home, to her surprise, was warm. It was also every bit as nice as she remembered it. 'How come the heating's on?' She headed straight for the kitchen to make coffee.

'Edward being thoughtful. He was here to meet your furniture van, remember?'

'I suppose they've put my stuff upstairs? I hope!'

Guy came up behind her. 'Why don't we go and check?'

There was a surprise for her. Once they had reached the second floor she realised why Guy had been anxious in case she'd changed her mind about which room she wanted to work in. Across the entire length of one wall, beneath the window, a work-bench had been built in, complete with shelves, drawers and compartments just like the one built in at the cottage.

'Guy! I don't believe it!'

'Believe it,' he smiled. 'I got Paul to organise it. Happy birthday, Elaine.'

'You remembered! I wasn't even sure whether you knew.'

'Twenty-three today,' he said, his arms sliding around her waist. 'And while I'm desperate for a cup of coffee, I'm more desparate to make love to you, birthday girl.'

It was ages before they got their coffee, turned seven o'clock. 'What time did you say we'd collect Jamie?' asked Elaine. 'It's already past his bed-time.'

'I didn't. I told Esther if we weren't there by six, we wouldn't come till the morning.'

'There's no need for you to come with me. You've got more than enough to do,' Elaine assured him.

'True. I'm going to make a start tonight, actually. The sooner the better.'

'As you wish. What about dinner? Is there any food in the house?'

'If there is, it'll be thanks to Anna. Take a look in the refrigerator.'

She looked at him, suddenly realising something. 'How come this place is clean and tidy when *Rosalie* was such a wreck?'

'Mrs Hurrell, my cleaner—she's a very pleasant character. Alas, she doesn't come daily, it's too far from where she lives. She comes once a week and spends the day, on Thursdays. You can change that if you want to, or fire her if you'd rather do the heavy cleaning jobs yourself.'

Elaine didn't bother answering that; she knew he was joking. This was a big house, and help once a week would be more than welcome. The running of the place would be easy enough; the kitchen was a work of art, equipped with every mechanical aid there was to be had. In the utility room there were two chest freezers—capacity for far more than two adults and one child—but they were both empty, switched off at the moment. 'I dread to think what you were feeding Jamie when you brought him home at weekends,' she muttered, amusing him because he hadn't had the benefit of her train of thought. 'Anyhow, I'll collect Jamie in the morning, if I can find my way to Esther's house, then I'll go shopping in a big way.'

'Money!' Guy tapped his forehead. 'That's one thing I haven't got round to organising—cheque books, a joint bank account.'

'I do have my own money, Guy!' She had an income, too, not only from the sale of her jewellery but also, and mainly, from Don Black, which would last until such time as he had paid her in full.

'That makes two of us,' he said lightly. 'So aren't we fortunate?' Obviously having no wish to make an issue of this, and not prepared to hear any argument, he went on, 'My account will be put into both names and you will use it for housekeeping and anything else you like. Anything at all. Money is no object. Enough said.'

Edward and Esther Richardson were in their early sixties, both sprightly, grey-haired, slender and small in stature. It made Elaine wonder about Helen. Chances were she had been petite; she must have been very much shorter than Guy. Chances were she had been dark, too. Jamie's hair was as black as his father's—had Helen's genes contributed to that black intensity? There were photographs of her in the Richardsons' house, plenty of them, but Elaine had studiously avoided looking at them the first time she had been there. There were no photographs of her in Guy's house—their house—but she didn't find that odd. She thought it was Guy being tactful. She was to learn otherwise.

She found her way to the Richardsons' with difficulty, getting lost once in spite of the excellent map Guy had drawn for her. She wasn't good with maps of any kind; her sense of direction was negligible.

'Ah, there you are, Elaine!' It was Edward who answered the door to her. 'We were beginning to think you'd decided to extend your honeymoon!'

'We thought nothing of the kind.' Esther was on his heels, smiling as Elaine stepped into the hall. 'Come in, dear. Don't be embarrassed by what Edward says. Honeymoon, indeed!' She shot a disapproving look at her husband. 'Elaine's marriage to Guy is one of convenience, she's told us that herself.'

It wasn't quite what she'd said. Nobody had been allowed to think it was love in bloom, but Elaine had never used the word convenience.

'Anyway, dear, how did the wedding go?' she was asked before she had a chance to comment. 'Smoothly, I hope. You do understand about our not being there, don't you? It's such a long drive to the north . . .'

'Yes, a very long drive. Of course I understand. And yes, it went smoothly, thank you. Where's Jamie?'

'He's next door. Mrs Grove's got her grandson staying at the moment, he's the same age as Jamie and they're playing together.'

'That's nice. Er—shall I go and fetch him or will you? Only I'm late getting here and I've got a heck of a lot of shopping to do.'

'You've time for a cup of tea though, surely?' Edward asked.

'I—yes, of course I have. Thank you.'

'Sit yourself down then, make yourself comfy.'

Elaine sat, unable this time to stop her eyes from wandering to the wedding photograph which had pride of place on the mantelpiece. Esther noticed at once. 'Did you wear white, Elaine?' she asked.

'Yes, I—a suit. Nothing fancy.'

The other woman got up, picked up the photo of Helen

and Guy and handed it to her. Elaine had no choice but to take it. 'Helen's dress had twenty-two yards of material in it; she had it made especially. It was beautiful, don't you think?'

'Yes, beautiful. It's a lovely photo.' It was. Helen had been very pretty, taller than her parents but still dwarfed by her husband. More so than Elaine was. And she had been dark; her hair was as black as Elaine's. Cross with herself, she handed the photograph back. Dammit, she was making comparisons herself now!

'Guy put all his photos of him and Helen away after she died; he couldn't bear to look at them any more. They'd been so happy together, you know,' Esther told her.

'What are you chattering about now, Esther?' Her husband was back with a tea-tray, and there was a ring to his voice which sounded like a warning to Elaine's ears.

'Elaine was interested to see Helen's wedding dress,' she said defensively. 'You wouldn't understand, Edward. Women are always curious about things like that, especially in these circumstances.'

Elaine left the house feeling depressed. It didn't last long. Jamie was beside her in her car, chattering away happily, looking forward to their shopping expedition, asking if he could help push the trolley round the supermarket. 'Gran always lets me,' he added.

Elaine answered that carefully. 'Yes, you can push the trolley. I'll be glad of your help. But, Jamie,' she added pointedly, 'it doesn't mean I'll always let you do things your gran lets you do.'

'I know that! And I do lots of things with you that I don't do with her.'

She could have kicked herself. Jamie had things sorted out, *he* wasn't making any comparisons. At least, none where he found her wanting. 'Like peeling potatoes?'

'Lots of things,' he said gleefully. 'Lots and lots and

lots. Ooh, it's going to be nice having you as my mother! Should I call you Mum now?'

Careful again. 'That's up to you, darling. Why don't you think about it for a bit?'

He said he would let her know, which almost made her laugh out loud, he said it so seriously. In truth, much as she adored Jamie, she herself would have to get used to the idea. She hadn't even got used to the fact that she was Mrs Harris yet.

There was a minor catastrophe in the supermarket. It was in Penzance, not a vast store but one that had everything she needed. Having no idea where best to shop, she had picked on this one because there was a parking space handy. It wasn't Jamie who caused her embarrassment, it was herself. Somehow she managed to do one of those things she'd always dreaded doing—she knocked over a pyramid of soup tins.

The clatter was dreadful, heads turned in astonishment as the things rolled this way and that across the floor. Jamie looked up at her, frowning, as if she'd done it on purpose. 'We'd better put them back, hadn't we?'

'Oh, darling, I wouldn't know how to begin!' She was already on her knees though, trying to stop the wretched tins from getting under people's feet.

'Please don't worry about it.' One pair of feet came to a halt in front of her. Elaine raised her head along the length of an immaculate, navy blue suit to find herself looking at an extremely handsome man of about forty.

Whether he registered her appreciation of his looks, she didn't know, but he was looking at her with open admiration. He held out a hand to help her to her feet. 'I'm Justin Galsworthy. I own the shop.'

She laughed as he held on to her hand and shook it. 'I'm Elaine Harris, and I don't think I dare set foot in it again!'

He smiled, waving an arm dismissively. 'I don't recall

seeing you around before . . .?'

Jamie intervened, coming unnecessarily to her defence. 'I'll help Elaine put the soups back!'

'Well now, I have seen *you* before, young man! You're a regular. Don't you normally come in here with your grandparents?' Mr Galsworthy was looking at Elaine as he asked the question.

'That's highly probable. It explains how he knows where everthing is!'

'At first glance I'd taken him to be your son . . .'

The remark pleased her. 'He's my stepson.'

'Ah, then it's *Mrs* Harris.' He glanced at Jamie again. 'Mrs Guy Harris.'

'Do you know my husband?'

'No, but I know of him. We don't have many celebrities living in the area.'

She fought a smile, knowing how Guy would dislike being referred to as such.

'To be honest, I hadn't heard that Mr Harris had remarried.'

'Less than a week ago, actually.' He was flirting with her, there was no doubt about it. In reply he murmured something short and unintelligible, but he let his eyes speak for him: pity about that.

His next words were delivered audibly and formally. 'Congratulations and best wishes, Mrs Harris. I look forward to seeing you in here again. Please don't bother about this lot, one of the staff will see to it.'

Even Jamie had noticed his admiring looks. 'He liked you, didn't he? I could tell! I bet he thought you were pretty.'

His powers of observation took her aback. He was a bright child, but she hadn't expected that. 'Well, I am!' she protested, sending him into gales of laughter.

Elaine began to get used to being addressed as Mrs Harris during the days leading up to Christmas—by the cleaner, and by the people in the local village shops, who somehow knew who she was before she told them. Shopping in the village for bits and pieces was handy, easier than driving in to Penzance now Christmas was so near.

She got used to that, and to being made love to nightly by Mr Harris. Almost nightly. Guy invariably got into bed long after she had retired, often in the dead of night, around three or even four a.m. More often than not she would wake, or he would wake her simply by putting his arms around her . . .

One morning, she woke early to discover she was alone, that Guy hadn't come to bed at all. Worried, she went in search of him. He was asleep on the settee in his study; it was a four-seater and it accommodated his length nicely. Still, it was hardly as comfortable as being in bed.

When she touched his shoulder, waking him, she said as much. 'Guy, you'll give yourself neck-ache sleeping like that!' She shouldn't have said anything, shouldn't have woken him. She quickly got the message that this was deemed as interference.

'That's the way it goes,' he told her. 'I sleep, I work, I work, I don't sleep. I crash out here for an hour. Whatever. You've got to respect that, Elaine. I normally go with the mood, but at the moment I have no choice. I can't spare much time for sleeping.'

She backed off gracefully, instantly. They had an implicit understanding in this respect, they always had: they did not try to manipulate, they didn't encroach on one another's privacy, freedom, life-style. 'Sorry. I just thought——'

'That I need a full night's sleep. You're right.' To her relief he grinned, catching hold of her by the waist. 'I do! I'll get one as soon as I can. What time is it?'

'Six. Five past six.'

'So that's why it's dark out there! Why are you up at six in the morning?'

'Because I missed you.' She smiled, moving away from him. He needed a shave. He needed a haircut—the black curls were running amok. He looked beautiful. 'There was no dent in your pillow and—I got worried.'

'Come back here. I'll soon fix that.'

'No. You're awake now so you might as well use your time constructively!'

'I said come here. You've woken me, you wretch, and I'm going to take advantage of it. You know full well you're a distraction. You can't walk in here wearing nothing but one of my old shirts and expect nothing to happen.'

'Then I'll be sure to buy a nightie or two today. Long ones. And a nice, modest dressing gown.'

'Red flannel?'

'If that's what turns you off.'

'Where's that effort Anna bought you?'

'Relegated to the back of the wardrobe,' she told him.

'Pity. I liked it.' He was looking at her naked thighs. 'But I think I like you in that old shirt more. There's less of it.'

Guy started work at eight that morning. When Jamie knocked on their bedroom door, he was still in bed with her, having a cigarette and a cup of coffee he had made in his study. He kept a kettle in there so he could make coffee when he wanted it, without having to be disturbed or to disturb himself with a trip to the kitchen.

Jamie flung himself on to the bottom of the bed when Guy called to him to come in. He had been told very firmly by his father that he was not to walk into the bedroom unless and until he was told he might. 'Are we going Christmas shopping today?'

'We are.' Elaine nodded vigorously. 'We'll have to go

into Penzance. I'm still searching for something specially nice for Anna.'

Guy lifted an eyebrow. 'As a thank you for the negligee?'

'What's a negligee?'

'In spite of the negligee,' Elaine retorted before explaining the meaning of the word to Jamie.

Anna Masters was rapidly becoming a firm friend. She and Paul had been over for a drink only once, thanks to Guy's pressing schedule, but Elaine had spent several hours with Anna at her home, times when she had taken Jamie to his grandparents and had left him with them for a couple of hours.

When Elaine had asked Anna not to avoid using Helen's name, the other woman had been obviously relieved. 'It isn't that Helen and I were great friends. Paul met Guy first, Helen and I got to know each other because of them. She kept herself very much to herself, as far as I know.'

'As far as you know?'

'By that I mean, if she had girl friends she saw during the day, I wasn't one of them. I saw her mostly in the evenings, if we all had dinner together or something.'

Elaine looked at her carefully. 'There's something else, isn't there, something you're not saying?'

Anna had denied that, but she didn't hold Elaine's steady look. 'No, it's just that I'm glad I haven't got to avoid mentioning her at all. It would be unnatural.'

'Absolutely. That was my point. It would be as bad as Esther *always* talking about her.'

Anna looked distressed. 'Does she? Oh, Elaine! Why don't you say something?'

'Like what?'

'Like—I don't know! Difficult, isn't it?'

'It's nothing I can't handle, not to worry. I do bear in mind that Helen was her only child, that her death must have been a terrible shock to her—and everyone else. She doesn't mean anything by it, doesn't do it on purpose, I'm sure of that.' It was true. Esther Richardson was in no way a malicious person, and she had no reason on earth to wish to hurt Elaine. So Elaine never mentioned it to Guy; she regarded it as her own problem. She didn't want him to know how much the mention of his first wife bothered her.

Elaine found the perfect gift for Anna that day with Jamie. A hand-knitted, fluffy angora sweater in pink, a colour she seemed to favour. Pastel shades went well with her dark blonde hair and she was a very feminine type.

Christmas and New Year came and went—not fast enough for Elaine. Christmas Day with the Richardsons was awful. Guy was quiet, obviously tired and tense because of the hours he was putting in on the final draft of his book. It was very nearly but not quite finished—which didn't please him. He still needed a few more days' work on it.

The day had begun well; watching Jamie's excitement with his presents on Christmas morning was a new experience for Elaine. He piled as many as his father would allow him to into the car before they set off to see his grandparents.

Esther and Edward had gone the whole hog: Christmas decorations, a big tree, enormous turkey with trimmings and all. They'd both worked hard and Elaine took care to remark on it, her praise for their efforts sincere. It might have been all right, the day might have gone quite well but for the few minutes which spoiled it in the early afternoon.

It wasn't that Esther mentioned Helen, on the contrary. It became obvious to Elaine that her husband must have said something to her even before the older woman actually came out with it and complained that he had.

The men were in the living-room with Jamie, Elaine was coming out of the bathroom when she was confronted by Esther. 'Elaine, I must have a word with you in private.' She was agitated. 'It's about—well, Edward says its wrong of me to mention Helen in front of you, he says you might think I'm comparing you with her. I told him that's ridiculous. It isn't that you could be jealous of someone who's—no longer living. I understand your situation far better than he does, I know you don't imagine you can take Helen's place in Guy's affections. You're far more down to earth than that, you're a very level-headed girl. Edward and I had quite a row about it, I told him if he expected me never to mention my daughter's name in front of you, he's asking too much.'

Elaine had never felt so awkward in her life. Esther was looking at her expectantly, waiting for her comments. She also looked upset. *What* could Elaine say? Esther Richardson was a kind, sweet person, and Elaine did not want to upset her. Nor did she want to antagonise her, since that would make for an awful atmosphere.

She used the same words Anna had used. 'I agree, it would be unnatural to expect you not to mention Helen.' She left it at that, hoping to get away without saying more.

She didn't. Esther put a hand on her arm. 'And it doesn't bother you, does it?'

It wasn't really a question, it was a statement. 'No, it doesn't bother me.' She smiled reassuringly, breathing a sigh of relief as Esther preceded her downstairs and into the living-room. End of conversation.

But Elaine's last words hadn't been true. It bothered her all right, it bothered her because in her heart of hearts she knew Guy was still in love with his first wife, that it was the memory of Helen which prevented him from loving her. He had come to terms with her death, as he had said, far more than Esther had, but that made no difference to his feelings. Elaine was only a substitute, one that he found physically attractive. Guy had never actually used the word 'convenience', either, although for him that was exactly what this marriage was—she had to face that.

The ripple of resentment she felt was quickly quelled. *Don't*, she told herself. Don't think like this. You knew exactly what you were getting into, it's too late to feel bitter now. You knew all you needed to know about Guy when you married him.

CHAPTER SEVEN

DURING the first week of January Elaine had reason to question the accuracy of that last thought. Guy had finished work on the final draft of his novel and had sent it off to his agent. There were a few days to go before location filming began on *Another Time, Another Life*. Fortunately this would not necessitate his being away from home—they were using the actual setting in the book, Black Head on Goonhilly Downs. It was within driving distance for Guy.

The other people involved with the production were staying at a hotel outside Helston. It was there that Guy spent a few days, in conference, immediately after New Year. He left home early and got back late . . . except on the Wednesday of that week.

Not realising he would be home early, Elaine stayed in town most of the day. She had seen some full-length sheepskin coats advertised in the January sales, which were just what she needed. The weather was bitterly cold now, and because of this she had asked Anna to have Jamie for the day. As it turned out, she wished he were with her, she missed him. Besides, her mood was extremely low that day and Jamie would have stopped her from dwelling on her thoughts. The shopping didn't.

She got home around four, just before it went dark. Finding the house ablaze with lights, she wondered what was going on. Nothing was going on. Guy was in the living-room, cigarette in one hand and a drink in the other. Elaine knew instantly something was wrong, what she didn't know was what, and why he was glaring at her.

'Where's Jamie?' he demanded. No greeting, nothing.

'He——' She broke off, smiling. 'And a good afternoon to you, too! Jamie's with Anna. I just called to collect him on my way home, but there's no one in. They must have popped down to the village or something.'

'And where have you been?'

'Shopping.' She was peeling off her layers of clothing: coat, hat, gloves, boots. 'Gosh, it's freezing today!' She turned, frowning. 'Why are you so grouchy? What's up?

'Supposing you tell me!'

'Guy?' His face was like thunder now, his grey eyes bleak with anger. 'Explain, please.'

'You explain!' he exploded. 'I come home to find the house empty, no note, nothing. Now you come home minus Jamie and tell me you've been shopping. Well, where is it? Where's the stuff you bought?'

Elaine couldn't believe her ears, her eyes. 'Good grief, what on earth's got into you?' She had made allowances for his tiredness for weeks now—since they got back from their honeymoon, in fact. Guy had worked like a dog and she knew it had to take its toll somehow. But this? She was at a loss. 'In the end I didn't buy anything. I was looking for a coat, a sheepskin. Oh, I don't know, I suppose I wasn't really concentrating. I've been a bit distracted all day.'

'Is that a fact?' His voice was nothing less than scornful, his American accent more pronounced than usual. 'What time did you go out this morning?'

Elaine lowered herself into a chair, utterly bemused. 'Nine o'clock.'

'So you've been shopping without buying anything the entire day?'

'What is this?' Irritation was making itself felt, caused by his attitude rather than anything else.

'It was a simple question. Answer it!'

'Are you asking me to account for my movements, Guy? If so, I'd like to know the reason.'

'Just answer the question, Elaine.'

'Very well,' she was holding on to her temper, still making allowances. 'I went to several shops, had lunch, and then I spent an hour in church.'

'In *church*?'

'Yes, in church!' She shot to her feet. 'It's one year today since my parents were killed, and that's the reason, before you ask!'

There was a sudden silence, crackling across the space that separated them. Elaine broke it, reasoning that his mood was foul because of something to do with his work. 'You—had a hard day or something, did you?'

He didn't answer. He was looking down at the carpet. Suddenly, swiftly, he stood and walked out of the room. 'I'll be in my study. Call me when dinner's ready.'

Elaine stared after him. He had given her the third degree for some reason, ignored her and then asked to be called when it was feeding time! What—who did he think she was, a maid?

She had a cup of coffee before ringing to see whether Anna was back. When she went to collect Jamie, she came straight out with what had happened, still unable to believe the way Guy had carried on. 'I've just had my first argument with Guy.' Jamie wasn't within earshot, he was in the playroom with Anna's daughter, Lucy.

'Lucky you.' Anna laughed. 'You've known him all this time and you've only just had your first argument? That's not bad!'

Elaine couldn't make a joke of it. 'I suppose not. But, honestly, I just had the feeling I didn't know him at all. It was like talking to a stranger.' This was met with a curious look. Anna asked what she meant.

'I got back to the house around four. Guy was home. I hadn't expected that. Anyhow, he—well, I don't know what he thought! He demanded to know where I'd been, what I'd been doing all day.' This time her words were met with silence, but she didn't miss the way Anna suddenly averted her eyes. 'Anna? What is it? Can you account for it? I've never seen Guy behaving so strangely.'

'He's been working too hard.'

'*Is* that it? It's what I thought, but . . .' Elaine didn't finish the sentence. There was something going through Anna's mind, but she wasn't going to say what it was. It disappointed her, gave her the feeling of being alienated. What did Anna know that Elaine didn't? Or was she imagining things? Pride wouldn't let her ask again. 'Well, I'd better take Jamie now.'

There was a look of apology on Anna's face. 'Elaine— look, don't worry about this. I haven't seen Guy for ages but I'll bet he's shattered. Make allowances, it'll pass.'

'Yes.' She brightened. 'He needs some relaxation— why don't you and Paul come over on Saturday? Have dinner with us? We can put Lucy to bed in one of the spare rooms.'

'Lovely! And while we're on the subject of getting together I want to be sure and book you for our anniversary party. It's a long way off, the first week in March, but I'm giving you and Guy plenty of notice so you'll have no excuse for not being there.'

'Anna! Of course we'll be there!'

'Good. We're giving a party on the Saturday, though our anniversary actually falls on the Sunday. Who gives a party on a Sunday?'

Paul got home then. He had a TV and video shop in Penzance, a thriving business which obviously made a lot of money, judging from their house and the cars he and Anna drove.

'Heavens, is it that time?' Elaine looked at her watch. She knew Paul never got home before six. It was six-forty. 'Hello and goodbye, Paul! Must dash. It's almost Jamie's bed time and I haven't even fed him yet!'

'I've fed him.' Anna was smiling. 'When we got in from the village. Chips and baked beans. Sorry about that! It's Lucy's favourite combination and——'

'Jamie asked for some.' Elaine nodded ruefully. She had got used to the things children liked to eat. 'Thanks, Anna. And don't forget, I'll be happy to reciprocate if you want a day's shopping by yourself.'

Paul was watching Elaine. She was still agitated in spite of her chatter. 'How's it going?' he asked casually. 'Being a mum and all that? You got thrown in at the deep end, didn't you?'

Elaine knew instantly that he had sensed something was amiss. Paul Masters was an astute and sensitive man. He was almost as tall as Guy but much heavier, the type she thought of as a gentle giant. He was a placid person who had no airs and graces, with a lot of charm in his own solid, down-to-earth way. She liked him enormously. 'No, Paul. *I plunged* in at the deep end.'

He inclined his head in acknowledgement.

'See you Saturday. You're invited to dinner.'

It wasn't until Elaine was driving home that she realised she shouldn't have issued the invitation without consulting Guy. Still, he wouldn't be working in the evening. They couldn't film in the dark, could they?

He was still in his study when she got in. Elaine got Jamie ready for bed, feeling loath to disturb his father, which in itself annoyed her. 'Come on, Jamie. We'll go in so you can say goodnight to Daddy.'

Guy wasn't working on anything. He wasn't doing anything. He was lying on the settee. Beside him was an overflowing ashtray and a fresh drink. His eyes went immediately to Elaine's and in them was an apology.

Over dinner he put it into words. 'I'm sorry about this afternoon. I guess I'm a bit uptight right now.'

Elaine thought before answering. The incident had ruffled her more than she had realised, but she didn't want to let it get out of proportion. 'That's okay. You're uptight because you need a rest. Perhaps you'll be able to have one when the filming's over. But, Guy, just for the record I don't like being asked to account for my time. That isn't . . . wasn't . . .' She stopped, tongue-tied. She had been about to say *part of our agreement*, but couldn't. It was distasteful to her. She loved Guy Harris more with every passing day. The trouble was that as the days passed she was becoming more demanding emotionally, in her head, her heart. She wanted him to love her, if not as much as she loved him, not as much as he'd loved Helen, then at least a little. Just a little.

Guy said it for her. 'It wasn't part of our agreement. Well, I've apologised, haven't I?' The words came out sharply. 'Do you want it in writing?'

Elaine had to get up for fear of his seeing the tears that sprang to her eyes. 'I'll get our dessert.'

The rest of the meal was silent, the atmosphere tense with unspoken words, their respective thoughts. After clearing away, Elaine went up to her rooms. She had got the second sitting-room just as she wanted it. Indeed she had sorted out her work-room, too. All in all, she thought she had coped very well during the time she'd lived here, what with the intervention of Christmas and all the shopping, getting to know new people, new surroundings, keeping an eye on Jamie almost constantly because Guy had been unable to. Jamie would start play school next week, three mornings a week. It was time for her to get down to work now, to start preparing some stock for the summer trade. Her work was soothing, something she loved doing; she had missed it. The thought of getting down to it was cheering, and heaven knew she needed cheering up right now. Her mind had been churning with thoughts of her parents all day. She could have lived without that scene with Guy, today of all days. She was wound up like a spring right now.

Guy stuck his head around the door before he turned in. 'I'm off to bed, Elaine. You working?'

'Not exactly.' She didn't turn to look at him. 'Just sorting out, seeing what I need to buy before I can get down to it.'

'Will you be long?'

The question infuriated her. Angrily, she twisted round in her chair. 'I see! It's okay for you to disturb me when I'm busy but not vice versa.'

'Hey! I simply asked——'

'Well, don't ask. It seems there's one set of rules for you and a different set for me. When did I ever ask how long you'd be? It's more than I dare do when you're involved with something!'

'What's bugging you? Hell, I apologised over this afternoon, didn't I?'

Elaine glared at him, for once unmoved by the sight of his large frame filling the doorway. Normally she only had to look at him to want him. Which, of course, was precisely why he wanted to know when she was coming to bed. Sex. She flung the accusation at him without stopping to think, without caring how he might react. 'What's the matter, Guy? Feeling sexy? Have you ever stopped to think how selfish you are? Have you never paused to think how much I've had to cope with these past few weeks? Of course you haven't! This household revolves around you, your work, your wants, your moods. Still, that's what you married me for—I'm your house-keeper and a surrogate mother for your child. I'm your problem-solver. I'm also your bed-mate. Well, not tonight, I'm not! *I* am not in the mood, so if you think you can come in here——'

If Guy had been angry earlier, it was nothing to how he was now. He crossed the room in two strides, yanking her violently to her feet. 'What the hell are you saying?'

'I'm saying you're selfish! I'm saying if you think you

can use me *all* the time to suit your own ends, you're wrong!'

'My God!' He shook her, shook her till her teeth rattled. 'Is that what you think? That I use you? Is that what you think I married you for? Just for my convenience?'

There it was again, that word. She wrenched away from him, dizzy from his rough handling. 'It certainly looks that way from where I'm standing!'

'What about this?' he demanded, pulling her tightly against him so her body was moulded against his. 'Do you feel *used* when I make love to you? Do you?' His laughter was not a pleasant sound. 'So you're not in the mood, eh?'

He kissed her brutally. It was absolutely the wrong thing to do at that moment. Elaine fought him, her hand coming up with the speed of light. It landed against his face with a resounding smack.

They stared at one another in silence. She couldn't believe what she'd done, couldn't believe they'd fought like this. Guy was looking at her in a way he never had before, his eyes registering astonishment ... and fury. Very quietly, frighteningly so, he said, 'If you ever try that again you'll get more than you bargain for—far more!'

She wouldn't try it again, ever. Not only had she shocked herself, she couldn't bear what she could see in his eyes. He thrust her away from him, looking as though he hated her. He might well. She hated herself. Why had she blown her top like that? Why had she needed to release the pressure inside her? Why was it there to begin with? What had he done, really?

The tears that were in her eyes brimmed over and slid down her face. 'Guy—oh, Guy, what's gone wrong?'

It was a second before he answered; she thought he never would. 'I don't know. It's me, my fault. I——'

'No! Look, I'm sorry for what I said, what I did . . .' He shrugged tiredly, turning towards the door. She panicked.

'No! Don't go!' She couldn't stand it. Dear Lord, she loved him so much. 'Guy, please! Kiss me. Kiss me, *please*. I can't, I don't——'

With a groan he wrapped her in his arms as she flung herself at him, kissing her violently, as if there were still some emotion he had to purge. They made love right there, on the floor, both reacting as if their need were desperate, as if it had been a long, long time.

When it was over, when she came to her senses, Elaine was shocked at herself again. It wasn't because she had behaved so wantonly—she always did. And Guy loved it. Whatever else was missing between them their sex life was hot, exciting to an extent which still amazed her.

But this had been different. For Elaine it had been a reaching out, an attempt to get close to him in more than the physical sense, to regain what they had had before, whatever that was. For Guy it had been lust—and lust alone. This was a new experience for her, knowing physical satisfaction and . . . emotional dissatisfaction. He wasn't even looking at her now, let alone holding her as he always had after making love; he had turned his back to her the moment their violent climax was over.

The element of caring which had always been present hitherto was missing now. Whatever they'd had before, insufficient though it was for her, it had been better than this. Quite suddenly she was uncomfortably aware of her partial nudity, self-conscious, something she had never been with him since their wedding day. Filled with a painful disquiet, she picked up her clothes, the items torn from her in their haste. She got up from the floor, her body stiff and aching. Lust, and lust alone, it left a bad taste in the mouth.

'If you were trying to show me the difference, Guy, you

succeeded.' It was barely more than a whisper, she was hurting physically, mentally and spiritually.

He didn't move, didn't look at her. 'Actually, I wasn't. I seem to recall your asking for it. I *don't* recall your behaving like one being used.'

It was the truth. Elaine headed for the bathroom without another word. Her traitorous body had negated the point she'd been trying to make. It seemed she was always ready to make love with Guy, regardless of the circumstances. Even when they'd fought bitterly. That was how much power he had over her. That was what it meant to be crazily, madly in love with him.

It seemed ages before Guy came to bed. Elaine lay in the darkness, wishing she could erase this entire day from her memory, wishing fervently she had never spoken in terms of being used . . . even though part of her felt it was true. For the hundredth time she reminded herself that she had known what she was getting in to. What she hadn't realised was how much it would bother her living in Helen's shadow. If only Guy could love her it would make all the difference in the world. As it was, she simply couldn't help this growing resentment she felt. Oh, it wasn't aimed at Guy, how could she resent him when he had never, ever, spoken in terms of love? He had never been false with her. It was just that she resented the—the *situation*. Resented herself, perhaps. She should have had more foresight, she should have thought ahead to the future, envisaged potential problems.

'Elaine?' Guy slipped into bed beside her. He hadn't turned a light on, he spoke very quietly. 'Are you awake?'

She dug her teeth into her lower lip. Should she feign sleep? She was so very close to tears. What she really wanted was to throw herself into his arms and tell him how desperately she loved him. But she had almost done that once tonight, she'd thrown herself at him and . . . it had all gone terribly wrong. 'I'm awake,' she said.

'We have to talk,' he said simply, the strain in his voice unmistakable.

Elaine closed her eyes tightly against the threatening tears. She couldn't trust herself to talk, not right now. If she attempted to she would lose control, blurt out all her worries and frustrations, tell him how she really felt about him. Ironically she loved him too much for that, too much to give him the responsibility of knowing her real feelings when he couldn't return them. It was bad enough that she'd said she felt used—to tell the whole truth would be disastrous. 'I know,' she said instead. 'But not now.'

They talked after breakfast the next morning, before Guy left for the day. Jamie was outside on his swing in the back garden, well wrapped up against the cold, though in fact the sun was shining, the sky clear.

His parents were watching from the window of the breakfast room. 'Where did he get that hat?' Guy asked. 'And how did you ever persuade him to wear it?'

Elaine smiled humourlessly. 'I know. He hates having his ears covered. I got it in town last week. We have a deal. If I allow him to play outside in this weather, it's on condition that he's armed against the cold. But he won't last long out there, you'll see.' She turned, her smile vanishing when she saw the intensity in her husband's eyes.

'Elaine, there are several things I must say to you.'

She was prepared. She didn't know what was coming, but she could cope, now. Things always seemed different in the cold light of morning. Yesterday was gone. She had lain awake for hours the previous night, thinking, trying to get things into perspective. She spread her hands, her voice calm and reasonable. 'Let me say one thing first, Guy. Yesterday was—I don't quite know what happened. Let's say I was particularly emotional because of the date. I'd been thinking about my parents, obviously.

My shopping trip was supposed to distract me. It didn't. And I'm sorry, I said things I didn't mean, I blew up.'

'You and me both. I was—in an odd mood myself. Our apologies aren't getting us anywhere, though. Words can't ever be retracted, not really. You know what they say, there's no smoke without fire. So tell me, are you unhappy?'

'No. I—no.'

'That won't do, Elaine. Say it. What were you going to add?'

She sighed, poured herself another cup of tea because she needed a few seconds in which to think, to consider her words. 'Just that I've needed time to adjust. My life's become very different very quickly.'

Guy seemed satisfied. 'I can't argue with that. The timing's been unfortunate, too. I've had no free time to spend with you or with Jamie. Or, ideally, with both of you together. We haven't had a chance to—to *be* a family, have we?'

She shook her head, wondering if they ever would be, could be.

'Well, I hope to change that in the near future. If you have felt you were being used——'

'Guy, try to forget I said that, please!'

'If you have felt used, I can't say I blame you. But that was *not* my intention. I want to make you happy, Elaine. Believe it or not, I want that very much. I want more than your not being *un*happy. When this filming's through, perhaps we can take that trip to Florida. We haven't discussed the future. We must at some point, but I can't really expect you to have an opinion on settling in Florida until you've been there.'

Elaine was concentrating on every word, but she wasn't actually looking at him. It didn't matter to her whether they stayed in England or settled in the States. All she wanted was to be with Guy. She had no emotional attachment to Cornwall. But what of him? 'Do you want to leave this house?'

'Not particularly, I like it very much, you know that. As I've told you, the only thing I have against England are the winters. Except for the year Jamie was born I've always gone back to Florida for a few months during the winter. But he'll be starting school full-time this fall, and that alters things, obviously. We can't shunt him back and forth, we'll have to decide where our permanent home is going to be.'

Elaine understood all that. It made perfect sense but ... 'I just thought that perhaps—I mean, doesn't this house hold too many memories for you?'

The question came casually, but Guy caught hold of her chin, forcing her to look in to his eyes. 'What are you really asking?'

She asserted herself. She was in no danger of giving too much away, and it was a reasonable question. 'I can't help wondering whether this house is a constant reminder of Helen?'

'I think of her from time to time, naturally. But the house has nothing to do with it.'

'And the one in Florida? It's another home you shared with her, during the winters.'

'The same applies, the answer's the same.' He let go of her, glancing at his watch. 'My surroundings don't haunt me, if that's what you're thinking.' He brought his eyes back to hers, narrowing them slightly. 'Ahh! I see where we're leading. You think the house keeps Helen in my mind. You wonder if I'm making a comparison between my two wives, is that it?'

Some of Elaine's control began to slip. She felt suddenly afraid. Afraid that if she were not careful she would oblige him to put into words that which she didn't want to hear. With as much nonchalance as she could muster, she admitted the thought had crossed her mind.

'Well, forget the idea. Wonder no more. You and Helen are like chalk and cheese. It's impossible to compare the two of you. Besides, what a fruitless pastime it would be! Helen is dead. I've told you before, I've come to terms with that long since.'

Elaine believed him, had believed it the first time he had said it. But it didn't help. His first wife still stood between them, still had the power to keep him from loving another woman.

'Do you dislike this house?' he went on.

'No, I love it.' It was the truth.

'So we won't rule out the possibility of staying on here?'

'Guy, I have an open mind, honestly. I don't mind where we live.'

'Great, that does simplify things.' He paused, considering her. 'It doesn't have to be Florida, either. We could live in California—anywhere in the States. All we have to do is make a decision.' He got to his feet. 'I have to go. You've answered the most important question. I woke up this morning wondering . . .'

'What?' His hesitation alarmed her. 'Wondering what?'

'Whether you thought you'd made a big mistake. After our discussion, I can see you're not thinking in those terms at all.' He smiled, a smile which made her want to scream in protest. He seemed convinced everything was fine again. Just like that. Oh, how straightforward everything must be to him! Elaine was by no means sure she hadn't made a mistake, the biggest mistake of her life!

Guy was about to leave, to say goodbye to Jamie, but the boy saved him the trouble. He came racing into the house, grumbling because it was too cold.

'And it's no fun playing by myself!' He looked up at both adults, his grey eyes so like his father's it never ceased to surprise Elaine. 'Why don't you have a baby?' he went on in his innocence. 'Now you're married you could get me a little brother or a sister, couldn't you?'

Elaine didn't know where to look. Guy was hardly comfortable with the question, either. He muttered something about 'wait and see', kissed Jamie goodbye and gave his wife what could only be described as a perfunctory peck.

She walked with him to the door, wishing they'd had time to talk on. If their conversation had satisfied him, it had not done the same for her. 'Guy——'

He cut her off. 'I know. Out of the mouths of babes. An awkward moment, was it not?'

'I—wasn't about to refer to that, actually.'

He looked at her directly. 'What then?'

'You don't—I mean, you don't feel you made a mistake, do you? If that is the case, there's no point in our going to Florida, no point in discussing a future together. For Jamie's sake it would be better to end——'

Guy's expression changed completely. His eyes darkened, making her think she had angered him again. 'No,' he said shortly. 'I wanted to be married to you, Elaine. If I hadn't, I wouldn't have gone through with it. I still want it. So the answer is no, I don't feel I made a mistake!'

'It's just——' It was no use, she knew she wouldn't be able to reach him, not without making a fool of herself and—and what had happened to her resolve? Last night in bed she had determined to make the very best of things. It was still early days. They had been married less than two months. Surely there was every possibility of improvement. He had just said he wanted to be married to her. What more could she ask, really, given all the circumstances?

She put a smile on her face. 'I was just going to tell you I've asked Anna and Paul to dinner on Saturday. I hope that's okay with you?'

'I'll look forward to it. Get on to that baby-sitting service. We'll take Anna and Paul out, save you the trouble of cooking.'

'No, it's no trouble.' Her heart sank. She hadn't convinced him, after all, she hadn't erased the complaint she had made, the damage she'd done. Why couldn't she learn to keep her big mouth shut, to count all the positive things in her life? She was expecting too much and it had to stop. 'It's no trouble at all. I'll enjoy making something special.'

'If you say so. Elaine, I must go, I'm running late as it is.'

CHAPTER EIGHT

NOTHING was the same from then on. That day in January changed things. Something, somehow, had been altered at a fundamental level. Their discussion, such as it was, had and hadn't helped. There was a shift in their relationship, a subtle change, negative in some respects and positive in others.

On the Saturday of that week Anna joined Elaine in the kitchen, ostensibly wanting to help. The children were in bed, the four adults had been talking and drinking for an hour, and everyone was starving.

There was nothing to do. Elaine had everything organised, the table set complete with candles and an arrangement of fresh flowers. She wasn't surprised when Anna asked how things were between her and Guy.

'You were upset the other day and I wasn't much help. It's just—well, I didn't really know what to say to you.'

'Don't worry about it.' Elaine smiled warmly, putting an arm around her. 'I put you on the spot. What could you say? You've known Guy far longer than you've known me. I don't expect you to take sides.'

'Takes sides? No, but——'

But what? It was happening again. What was it Anna wanted to say but felt she couldn't? 'Forget it, Anna. We talked it through the following morning, decided we'd both been in peculiar moods. Here you are, if you want to make yourself useful, take this wine and ask Guy to open it, would you?'

Anna took the bottle, keeping her voice low, not that they were in danger of being overheard. The men were talking in the living room, deep in disussion about some world-shattering event, by the sound of it. 'You love him very much, don't you?'

Elaine almost dropped the dish she had just picked up. She looked stricken.

'There's no need to look so horrified. I'm a woman, too, remember? I know precisely how you feel. For heaven's sake, you didn't think you had me fooled, did you? Guy might be too blind to see it, but I'm not.'

'Anna——'

'Relax! I'm not about to enlighten him, if that's what you're worried about. I'm not stupid, Elaine. You have a lot of sorting out to do, both of you. It's going to take time. All I want to say is—well, I've become very fond of you and I hope it works out. I feel sure it will. So please tell me, how are things, really?'

Elaine couldn't tell her. Anna was very likeable, but she was the wrong person to open up to. She couldn't be objective, could she? It wouldn't even be fair to expect it of her. In any case, this was hardly the time to find out. 'Not bad at all. Honestly. As you say, we have a lot of sorting out to do and it's going to take time.'

Time. January became February, bringing even colder weather. By then, life had slipped into a routine which should have made everyone happy. Jamie was going to play-school, Elaine was back to working, part-time, and Guy was on the brink of having some freedom. His involvement in the filming of *Another Time, Another Life* was all but finished. Soon he would have a chance to rest, have time on his hands.

They had spoken again about Florida, had decided to go there at Easter. They'd spoken about it only briefly, achieving no more than fixing a date. In reality, communication between them had disintegrated. They were both ... cautious now, both careful with their choice of words. It did not make for spontaneity. Time and again Elaine wished she had never had that outburst; she and Guy had lost what closeness they had had. They communicated only at a physical level, in what she now thought of as sex rather than lovemaking. It was no longer the same—it hadn't been since that awful day. There was a missing dimension. She didn't know how else to think of it, what else to call it. Dimension, element, whatever—it was missing.

Guy was no more able to resist her than she could resist him. Just being in bed together was a turn-on, regardless of anything else. But he no longer held her, cuddled her to sleep afterwards. Nor did she try to change that. To manoeuvre herself into her husband's arms when he was not so inclined would be like begging him to love her, or at least to demonstrate some feeling for her.

And yet . . . in other ways he did show he cared. In other ways he took the trouble to make her feel appreciated. He offered to cook now and then, he insisted on taking her out to dinner at least once a week. Perversely, it served only to sadden Elaine. Guy was determined not to allow her to feel used, was making a concerted effort to be an attentive husband. To her, it felt like what it was, duty. Sometimes she wanted to scream in frustration.

It didn't occur to Elaine that Jamie would be so aware of the atmosphere between her and Guy. She had no experience with children; it had been a long, long time since she had been one. She had forgotten how sensitive children could be.

One morning during breakfast in the middle of February, quite out of the blue, Jamie made a statement which both shocked and upset her.

He began bravely, almost matter-of-factly. 'Elaine, I *was* going to call you Mum, but I changed my mind.'

Elaine and his father exchanged looks. She loved her stepson dearly, and it would have pleased her to be addressed by him as Mum, but she hadn't wanted to influence him either way. She had never mentioned this subject to Jamie since they had had their little chat about it. She had left him to make up his own mind, as agreed.

'Why is that, son?' Guy asked casually. 'Is there any special reason?'

'Yes.' The child's voice wobbled as he went on. 'Elaine might not stay with us, Daddy. I don't want to call her Mum if she's going to leave us.' He looked at her. 'I don't think you like it here. You don't laugh like you used to, it isn't fun like it used to be. And you don't smile any more, Daddy. I——'

He couldn't go on. His eyes welled up with tears which overflowed and streamed down his face. Elaine put her hand to her mouth, appalled, wanting to cry with him. Of course she didn't, she reassured him immediately, as did Guy.

'Of course I'm staying with you, darling!'

'Elaine and I have been working too hard, that's all. We're just a bit tired.'

'You mustn't think for one moment that I'll leave you. How could I? You're my very favourite person in all the world. I love you, you goose!'

The tears abated somewhat. 'Wh-what about Daddy?'

Oh, Lord, how did she answer that one? She didn't. She nodded frantically, smiling what must have been an idiotic smile to his father's eyes. Worse, Guy was looking at her, not in the least amused, waiting to see what she'd say. 'He's one of my favourite people, too. Of course he is.'

'I'll tell you what,' Guy went on, 'we'll all do something fun together today. Elaine and I will collect you from play school later and then we'll go out and have something nice to eat. And then we'll go to the zoo. Lucy can come too, if her mum says it's all right. How does that sound?'

It worked. Between them they had stopped the tears,

had reassured him. The relief in that achievement was ruined, however, moments later. Jamie went off to fetch his coat and Guy turned to Elaine, apologising for his presumption. 'I put you on the spot, I'm sorry. I'll take him to play school today, you can at least have the morning to yourself and, well, I don't want to spoil any plans you might have for this afternoon, but I felt——'

'*Plans?*' She couldn't believe it. 'Like what?'

'Like all sorts of things. You might have wanted to work, or go out scouting for customers. That's what you've been doing these past few days, isn't it?'

She just looked at him, unable to believe he could think for one moment that she would put her work before Jamie.

'Well?' he asked with a sudden harshness. 'Isn't that what you've been doing while you've been out alone?'

'You know damn well it is! So what? I have no fixed routine. Jamie's more important than work or anything else!'

Guy opened his mouth to say something, but he changed his mind.

'I'm certainly not going to have you explain my absence when you pick him up from school,' Elaine went on. She was at a loss to understand him. *Again.* 'Are you crazy, Guy? After what we've just promised, that would serve to confirm all his fears!'

Guy got up from the table, picked up his car keys. 'I'm not altogether sure they're unfounded,' he muttered.

Elaine started clearing the breakfast table. Jamie's words went round and round in her head. How could she not have realised how insecure he was feeling? God knew she felt insecure! But Jamie hadn't shown it, hadn't said anything until today. He was a good little boy and she had believed he was happy. Well, he wasn't.

That made three of them.

Anna didn't probe further as to how things were. As

the day of her anniversary party drew closer, she made only one comment, and it was a suggestion Elaine wouldn't consider for even a second. It came unexpectedly one morning when Elaine was collecting Lucy to take her to the play school with Jamie. The two women normally took turns each, alternate weeks. It was actually Anna's turn but she was so busy with preparations for Saturday's party that Elaine had told her to skip it.

'How's it going?' Elaine had offered to help make the food, dishes which could be made in advance, but Anna had declined. She was going to spend the afternoon with Anna on Saturday, though, to help with last minute things. There were to be sixty-odd guests—at the last count.

'I might ask you the same thing.' Anna bundled her daughter into Elaine's car, closing the door before Elaine could get in. 'Hang on a moment,' she said quietly. 'Elaine, I know it's none of my business, but I can't keep quiet any longer. Guy looks more strained since he's stopped working than he did when he was breaking his neck over it.'

'I'm aware of that——' His having free time wasn't helping things at all. He took Jamie out and about by himself most of the time, leaving Elaine to get on with her work in peace. It was another instance of his being thoughtful, his doing what he thought he should do, what he thought she expected of him. Doing his share.

It wasn't helping matters one iota. Their lives, they themselves, were becoming too separate ... almost mechanical.

'As for you,' Anna went on, 'you're so tense you look fit to snap. Look, love, has it occurred to you it might be a good start if you did tell Guy how you feel?'

'Anna!'

Anna held up a hand. 'No. I've told you, I won't

interfere. It's just a suggestion. Is it such a bad one? *Is* it? You might be pleasantly surprised, Elaine.'

'What's that supposed to mean?'

'I mean maybe Guy feels the same way. Did that ever occur to you?'

'No, it didn't!' Elained snapped, apologising immediately. She was tense, it was true. It was obviously beginning to show. 'I'm sorry, but no, it hasn't. For all my faults, and God knows I'm stupid in some respects, I'm basically a realist.'

Anna moved away, her smile reflecting her sympathy, her own unhappiness with the situation. 'See you Saturday.'

On Friday the Harris family had lunch with Esther and Edward Richardson. It was something they did regularly but not too often. Elaine took Jamie for visits, dropping him off while she went shopping, and it was working satisfactorily. The veneer of friendship Esther had shown from the start had become genuine, Elaine was sure of that. She withstood any mention of Helen's name, telling herself it was her own paranoia when it irked her. She had never mentioned this to Guy, never told him how it rankled, that she thought it tactless but was powerless to stop it.

But it no longer mattered. This was one thing, at least, which she really had managed to put into perspective. Her reaction to Helen's name all stemmed from her own insecurity, she had realised. It was her problem and no one else's.

In any case it wouldn't irk her today. Esther rarely mentioned her daughter's name in front of Guy these days, and Elaine took that as another positive sign; his mother-in-law had adjusted to his re-marrying.

So if not to Anna and, no doubt, to Paul, at least to the Richardsons everything seemed all right between Guy and Elaine.

Edward and Esther had finally booked their world cruise. That was their big news, which they had hinted at when phoning to ask Guy and family over. Both were excited, extremely so, and Elaine was very pleased for them. She enthused over the brochures they showed her, asking sensible questions and generally sharing their good mood. When it seemed appropriate she mentioned that she and Guy were going away, the Florida trip at Easter. She had put off mentioning it until now.

She braced herself, both interested and worried at what their reaction might be. They couldn't miss the implications.

They didn't. But they didn't look overly disappointed, either, much to Elaine's relief.

'Does this mean you're going to reconnoitre, as it were?' Edward wanted to know. 'With a view to settling there, perhaps?'

'Perhaps,' Elaine said carefully. 'But only perhaps.'

Esther was looking at Jamie. 'Goodness, I'll miss you if you do go to live in America!'

Jamie seemed more upset than they at the prospect. 'You'd visit!' he told his grandparents, turning immediately to Elaine for confirmation.

'Of course they would, darling!'

'You couldn't keep us away.'

'At Christmas?' the child persisted, turning to his father this time.

'At any time Gran and Grandad wanted to come,' Guy assured him. Looks were exchanged all round. That idea was fine with everyone.

Guy remarked that night on how easy it had been. He and Elaine had just finished watching an excellent play on TV, the log fire was burning in the hearth, the lights were low, the mood mellow, for once with no sense of strain.

Elaine looked at him hopefully, wishing she were

sitting nearer to him. It was difficult to read his eyes from where she was. 'It was a relief, wasn't it? It's worried me, I'll admit. You're sure they weren't just being brave? I mean, taking it well because they were so bouyant to begin with?'

'I know exactly what you mean. No, it was a genuine reaction, they know they'd be welcome whenever they wanted to visit. They're not short of money and they have plenty of time on their hands, so there'd be nothing to stop them.'

'Guy, I've been thinking about——' The phone rang. Elaine was furious. It was rotten timing. For a minute she had hoped she and Guy were going to talk, really *talk*.

He motioned her to where he was standing. 'It's Don Black, he sold *Rosalie* today. He wants to talk to you.'

She had gathered it was Don, but not that he had sold the house. 'Don! How lovely to hear from you! Congratulations on selling the house. Yes, fine, just fine. And you?'

The conversation went on. They had had no contact with Don since their wedding day. He wanted to know all the news and, naturally, she wanted to ask him how things were at Faraday & Faraday. To her dismay, in the middle of her talking to Don, Guy waved briefly from the doorway and went to bed.

He was asleep when Elaine joined him. At least he appeared to be. Nothing happened. She was careful not to disturb him, to stay on her side of the bed. Whether he was asleep or not, it made no difference. What mattered was that he wanted her to think he was.

She lay perfectly still, her mind jammed with worries, questions. This was like the early days, nights, the nights shortly after she'd met Guy, when she had speculated and puzzled over him. She thought she had got to know the man well. How ironic that now, three months after their marriage, she felt she didn't know him at all. She closed her eyes, recalling that at the very beginning she'd thought Guy a man of contrasts. These days he was a man of moods, odd moods.

Why had he come up to bed when they were in the middle of a conversation? Why couldn't he talk to her? Why couldn't she talk to him? What had gone wrong, and at what point, exactly? Had their relationship been spoiled by marriage? Did that happen to some couples?

Couples? They were not and never had been a couple in the accepted sense of the word. But ... they had been good together, once. She wasn't fooling herself in thinking that, was she? It was hard to remember precisely how things had been before that stupid fight in January. Except that Guy had been working very hard. She'd seen so little of him, it was hard to tell how things were. But there hadn't been this much strain, they hadn't lain in bed avoiding one another, that was for certain.

It was easier to remember further back, back to last summer when they had been so very comfortable together, when they'd talked and laughed and teased. Jamie had been right that day when he had cried and spoken of his fears. Four and half years old and he had put it in a nutshell: there wasn't any fun now. Daddy didn't smile any more.

What a mess! And there was more irony: Guy had been instrumental in helping Elaine sort out her life last summer. He had bought *Rosalie* and all its contents, he'd been a friend, had listened and advised her about selling the business to Don. And then he had asked her to marry him and she had accepted knowing she was going, put at its most basic, to help him straighten his life out.

And where were they now?

What was happening to them?

What had gone wrong?

CHAPTER NINE

PAUL and Anna's party was a roaring success. Elaine was determined to enjoy herself . . . and she drank too much too fast in the effort. Still, the effect seemed beneficial: she loosened up, chatted a lot, laughed and generally got in to the swing of things.

The same couldn't be said for Guy. Tension was stamped all over him. On the other hand he didn't exactly like parties. He was cornered for the first hour by three women from the village, being bombarded with questions and treated like a celebrity, no doubt. Or maybe they simply fancied him. Elaine didn't go over to find out. There was one unaltering fact about Guy: he was not aware of his own attractiveness.

Unfortunately Justin Galsworthy was. He put in an appearance quite late, some time after ten, and after his first drink and an exchange with his host and hostess, he made a bee-line for Elaine.

She still shopped in his supermarket, never having found a reason to buy elsewhere. Since that first embarrassing day when she had knocked over the soup tins, there had been several occasions when she'd chatted to him. He wasn't always in the shop. He had several other supermarkets dotted around the area. Elaine had learned that much, and that he was a bachelor. That he found her attractive, she had known from the beginning.

It was merely a game to her. She thought him both astute and shallow, extremely good-looking and well aware of it. In all honesty she couldn't actually decide whether she liked him or not. Consequently she had always treated him with neutrality, as she attempted to tonight. But they were in a different setting, different circumstances. Elaine was merry and he was intrigued. Tonight, her neutrality seemed to challenge him.

'We-ell, who have we here?' His opening gambit brought a mocking smile to her lips.

'Little Red Riding Hood. And how are you, Justin? Still making a fortune?'

'One tries, one tries. You're looking gorgeous, Elaine. Now that's not the sort of dress you'd wear to visit your grandmother, surely?'

'No, but it is the sort of thing wolves are attracted to.' How right she was. She was wearing the classic little black number bought especially for the occasion, in velvet, cocktail length with tight sleeves and a plunge neckline. 'Justin, if you could possibly drag your eyes away from my breasts, perhaps you'd get me another drink?'

No sooner had she said this than she regretted it. She put her hand to her temple, watching as Justin moved away quickly to do her bidding, his smile outrageous and—almost smug. Somehow or other he had taken it as a come-on. What was the matter with her? The man was almost a stranger, really. Moreover, she was a respectable married woman. Unhappy, perhaps, desperately in love, God help her, worrying constantly over the past, the present and most especially the future, true. But married just the same.

Worse, Anna had heard her remark. She was standing with two people Elaine didn't know and she turned, her expression shocked to begin with, become a warning seconds later. She spoke in a hiss from the side of her mouth. 'You're being watched, be very careful, love.'

Watched? By whom? Guy! On the far side of the room, a head taller than the people he was talking to, he was staring at her as if he had heard what she'd said. Which was impossible.

Mutinously she looked away. Not tonight, *not tonight*. He was not going to depress her, to spoil her fun tonight.

'Here you are, beautiful.' Justin was back, his facial expression unchanged. 'So tell me—and don't give me that polite answer you gave me once before—how's married life?'

'I wouldn't recommend it,' she heard herself say. She didn't get any further. Anna immediately interrupted.

'Hello again, Justin. How's business, by the way? Paul's finding things very quiet at the moment, I think anyone who was going to buy a new TV or video did so before Christmas.'

'Quite so. But people have to eat all year round, so—okay! My shops are quite busy.'

Anna's hand dropped on to Elaine's shoulder, her fingers squeezing imperceptibly. 'I'm going to drag you away. I want you to meet two other illustrious shopkeepers!'

Elaine hesitated. The devil was in her. 'I'll join you in a moment, Anna.' There was another squeeze. Another warning. Well, to hell with it! 'In just a moment,' she said firmly.

As far as Justin was concerned, it was a green light. Elaine did not expect what followed, but she handled it well enough. 'So,' he smiled, his eyes sliding to her neckline again. 'When am I going to see you alone? Your husband has a reputation as a workaholic. I believe he's also something of a recluse. Life must get pretty boring for you.'

Elaine sobered. She hadn't expected such bluntness, but she had asked for this and she wasn't proud of herself. 'Boring? Never!' That, at least, was the truth. 'As a matter of fact, Guy isn't working on anything just now. And I wouldn't call him a recluse—he's over there.'

Justin didn't turn to look. Nor was he put off. 'I envy him,' he said baldly. 'He has not only a beautiful wife but

... a faithful one, too?'

'Totally.' She laughed a little. If she could keep this on a jokey footing, all would be well. People did flirt at parties, it was usually meaningless, just par for the course.

When Anna interrupted yet again, Elaine was relieved this time. No sooner had she been introduced to the two shopkeepers than Guy was by her side.

'Forgive me,' he said to the others, his eyes belying his smile. 'Must have a word with my wife.' His hand closed around Elaine's upper arm so tightly she almost yelped. He steered her into the hall, giving her no chance of escape.

Rage surfaced in her, suddenly, overwhelmingly. 'Let *go* of me! My God, I'll be black and blue tomorrow! What the hell do you think you're doing?'

'I'm taking you home.'

'*What?*'

'You heard.'

'Oh, I heard, all right. Goodnight, Guy. If you want to go home, you go right ahead! *I'm* staying. It isn't even midnight yet!'

In a tone she had never heard from him before, with a bitterness that left her open-mouthed, he said, 'And I'm very much afraid of what you might have turned into by the time the clock strikes twelve. So get your coat. Now!'

For two seconds Elaine stared at him, completely at a loss. Then she turned on her heel and walked back into the main room of the house, quickly, without another word or a backward glance.

He didn't pursue her. Nor did she stay long afterwards. The scene with Guy had ruined the party for her. It had also puzzled her. All right, he'd seen her talking to Justin Galsworthy but—firstly, he couldn't possibly have heard anything they'd said, and secondly, why such extreme behaviour? To demand that she leave their friends' anniversary party so early was unreasonable, an insult to them.

'If you'll take my advice, you'll go home.' Elaine turned to find Anna by her side. 'Go home, and for goodness sake, *talk* to him. He's upset.'

'*He's* upset? What——'

'Elaine, take my advice, please!'

Elaine sighed. What sparkle there had been in the evening had gone. Guy. Nothing mattered more than Guy. 'I—yes, I will. I'll do that. I'll go home and I swear it, I'll talk to him.'

'I'll get Paul to run you——'

'No. Absolutely not. I won't have him leaving the party, Anna. I'll walk, I need the air—come to think of it, I really do.'

'But it's pitch black out there!'

'And it's only half a mile. I know the roads well. I'm not going to get raped or murdered in a lovely, respectable area like this, am I?'

'Well, no, but——'

'Enough said. Goodnight. And I'm sorry. This shouldn't have happened here, most especially tonight.'

It was no surprise that Justin pursued her. He appeared outside the front door as if by magic.

Elaine refused his offer of a lift before he had a chance to make it. 'No, Justin. No way, thanks all the same. I want to walk.'

'That's ridiculous! It's freezing——'

It was hardly freezing; it was early March and windy but dry. 'I want to walk,' she repeated. 'And that's the way it's going to be.'

'What's the matter with hubby? Why the sudden departure?'

She sighed. She had allowed things to get out of hand, and she had to rectify that now. Very firmly. 'I really have no idea. Besides, it's none of your business. Do I make myself clear, Justin?'

'Perfectly,' he conceded, inclining his handsome head
with nonchalance. 'But if you ever change your mind,
you know where to find me.'

Elaine set off on her trek.

Her home was in darkness. Either Guy had simply
been thoughtless in turning every single light off, or he'd
decided she would stay over at Anna's, being without a
car. Jamie was staying the night at Anna's along with
two other guests' children.

She let herself in to the house as noisily as she could,
switching on lights as she went. He couldn't possibly be
asleep. He hadn't been gone that long. 'Guy?' Like an
idiot she kept calling his name. He wasn't home. It was
obvious, but it didn't stop her calling out to him. His car
was outside, but . . . Guy wasn't in.

Elaine stood, looking at their bed and wondering what
to do. Maybe he'd gone for a walk. To cool off. She had
no idea why he had been so disproportionately angry, but
she intended to find out. Life was becoming unbearable,
the tension was so bad it was changing her personality,
she *had* to talk to him. Even with Jamie she had been
snappy once or twice this past week. Darling Jamie. He
was innocent, it was unfair and unhealthy to be like that
with him. Happily, he'd hardly noticed; he had merely
frowned at her when she'd been short with him. She
always made a point of chatting to him at bedtime,
finishing the day with kisses and cuddles which were
reassuring to a little one.

Kisses and cuddles. She was still looking at the bed,
wondering whether or not to get in it. She went to the
bathroom, opened the door and stopped in her tracks.
There were twin basins in their bathroom, a large
cabinet, several shelves. All Guy's things had gone. No
comb, no razor, toothbrush—nothing at all.

Devastated, she sank on to the side of the bath,

convinced her legs wouldn't support her any longer. Which room had he moved into? What did it matter? He'd gone.

From bad to worse to . . . the beginning of the end. *Separate bedrooms.*

Panic took hold. Elaine raced out of their rooms, along the corridor, and hammered on the one bedroom door which was closed. 'Guy? Guy!'

She tried the handle. It was locked. Locked, for heaven's sake! *'Guy!'* she called.

'Get away from there, Elaine! Leave me in peace. I've had as much as I can take, do you *hear* me?'

Oh, how swiftly her emotions swung these days! From despair to panic to rage. In a flash. '*You've* had enough? How dare you? *How dare you?*'

The door swung open so fast, so suddenly, she fell against him. Her hands came out, balancing her by pushing against his chest. He was half undressed, wearing only his slacks. Elaine was wild with anger, anger and the pent-up frustration of months. It all happened in one movement, her steadying herself, her slapping him viciously. 'You bastard! Don't you think——'

The world turned upside down. Elaine was lifted bodily off the floor, turned almost completely upside down and bellowed at. 'I warned you! Don't say I didn't warn you, my *darling* wife! *Wife,*' he roared. *'Wife!'*

He had gone mad—she was convinced of it. He was carrying her down the corridor, flinging her on to their bed. It dawned incredibly slowly. It was seconds before she realised his intent, and even then she didn't believe it . . .

She fought, she cried, she thrashed out at him but what hope did she have against a giant of a man with six times her strength? Mercifully it didn't last long. Sanity returned, Guy stopped abruptly, jerking away in disgust to leave her lying there, shocked into silence.

On his way out of the room, he slammed the door so hard that the entire house seemed to reverberate.

Elaine lay where he left her, stunned beyond thought.

CHAPTER TEN

THE ability to think had returned by morning. Thinking was easy now ... but last night didn't bear thinking about. That Guy had come so close to ... no, is just did not bear thinking about. There was only *one* thought to think, one thing she had to do. One option only.

She was going to leave Guy. Today. Now.

She felt nothing, no emotions at all. Calmly she washed, dressed and went downstairs in search of her husband. She would tell him immediately, without preamble, that she was about to pack her clothes. There would be no post-mortem, no argument.

There wasn't any argument: Guy wasn't in the house. Elaine searched from room to room before it occurred to her to look outside. The Porsche wasn't there, nor was it in its garage.

Deflated, she sat at the top of the stairs. Jamie. Guy must have gone to collect Jamie from Anna's house. She looked at her watch. It was turned eleven. How had she managed to sleep so long, to sleep at all? Everyone had probably overslept after the party.

She went back upstairs, she might just as well start packing right now.

It didn't take long to fill a case, to fling in enough clothes to see her over a few days. She would go to a hotel. No, she would drive to the north. Or maybe she would go to London and stay with her cousin for a few days, till she sorted herself out, decided what to do. All that mattered for now was getting away. Enough was enough.

She took her case downstairs, dumped it in the hall and looked again at her watch. Where were Guy and Jamie?

There was only one way to find out.

'What's the matter?' It was Paul who came on the line. He didn't answer her question about Guy. 'Elaine, what is it? You sound strange.'

'I'm—nothing, Paul.' The gentleness in his voice was upsetting her, dispelling her state of shock. She resented that, it was better not to feel anything. Nothing hurt then. 'I just want to know whether Guy's there. Please tell me!'

'Take it easy. There's no mystery about it, you know! No, we haven't seen him. Elaine, what is it? Come over here, please.'

'I—yes, I'll have to.' Jamie. She couldn't leave without explaining things to Jamie—without *trying* to. Oh, God! What was she going to tell him? He wasn't yet five years old, how could he possibly understand? *How* was she going to tell him, come to that? Only a few weeks ago she had promised never to leave him, had told him she loved him. How was she going to explain that that was still true, that she loved him but had to leave him?

She arrived at her neighbours' house to find Jamie and Lucy wearing hats, coats and gloves. Paul had his coat on, too. 'I'm going to take the children for a drive,' he said cheerfully.

Catching the look in his eyes, Elaine responded accordingly, forcing herself to smile. She couldn't speak. She was on the verge of breaking down. Jamie was looking up at her, sensing something was wrong, frowning in that way he had when her behaviour was puzzling to him.

'Elaine and I are going to have a nice chat while you have your drive.' Anna's hand came to rest on her shoulder, gently this time. Reassuringly. 'These two have been ever so good, Elaine, helping with the tidying up.'

Elaine blinked, looking around for the first time. The house had been restored to order.

'So maybe,' Paul said with a twinkle, 'just maybe I'll buy them lunch while we're out, as a special treat.' Over the children's hoots and exclamations of delight, Paul looked at his wife. Quietly, with uncharacteristic sternness he said, 'Tell her, Anna. *Tell* her, because if you don't, I will!'

Nothing was said until the two women were alone. Elaine collapsed into a chair, and Anna sat facing her. 'What happened when you got home last night?'

Elaine was shaking her head from side to side, unable to speak.

'I take it you had a row?'

'Not exactly.' It was no more than a whisper. 'It was worse than that. I can't . . . won't talk about it. Anna, I'm leaving Guy. Today!' She broke down, head in hands, sobbing for all she was worth. She cried as violently as she had when her parents had been killed. This felt similar: she was losing two people she loved.

'*Leaving him?* Oh, no! Elaine, *no*! You can't do that!'

'Just—just watch me.' Elaine's voice was pathetic. She lifted her head, took the box of tissues Anna was handing to her. 'Poor Anna, you look as unhappy as I am.'

'With good reason! I'm very fond of both you and Guy and I can't stand by and watch this happen. Elaine, he loves you, don't you know that?'

'Loves me? You poor fool! Get down off that cloud, will you? Guy doesn't love me. He never has and never will. He's still in love with Helen.'

'Rubbish! What utter rubbish!'

Elaine's hands were thrashing about in frustration. How could Anna understand, why should she? 'You don't know how it is. All you know is what you see. You don't live with Guy, I do. You don't understand him like I do. He's——' She stopped abruptly. What was she saying, that she understood Guy? It was hardly accurate. He had turned into a stranger. They had been married precisely three months and in that time he had changed beyond recognition.

Very quietly Anna said, 'Quite. Now listen, I have something to tell you. It might help you understand him.'

'It makes no difference now. Nothing you say will change my mind.' Elaine was thinking about last night. 'I believe I've stopped loving him. Anna, I think I actually hate him!' A fresh bout of sobbing brought her friend to her side, had Anna's arms going tightly around her.

'Stop that! Come on now, stop it! You've got it all wrong, love. I—I've wanted to tell you before, but I didn't think it right. Neither did Paul, until last night. We don't believe in interfering—we were both convinced Guy would tell you this himself but it's obvious he never has.'

'Tell me what? What is it?'

'About Helen,' Anna said dully. 'Her unfaithfulness.'

'*What?* I can't——'

'Believe it?' Anna smiled humourlessly. 'Believe it, love. Helen had been having an affair for years. Behind Guy's back, of course. That's what last night was all about. Guy was jealous, angry, insecure—all of those things.'

Elaine was stunned. Her tears stopped, she sat motionless, trying to breathe evenly. 'Are you telling me Helen had an affair with Justin Galsworthy?'

Anna laughed shortly. 'Good grief, no! Don't be silly. You don't think I'd have invited both of them into my house if that were the case! Guy would have done much more than walk out, believe me!'

'Then who . . . how . . .?'

'I don't know the man's name. Neither does Guy. Well, he knows his first name. He—never tried to find out more. It was too late by then. Irrelevant.' She looked up, apologising. 'I'm sorry, I'd better start at the beginning. I—actually, there isn't that much I can tell you, you'll have to hear the full story from Guy.'

'There's not much chance of that.' But there was hope. There was hope, wasn't there? All this time she had believed Guy's marriage to Helen had been one of those made in heaven. Ideal, perfect! And now . . . 'Tell me what you can, Anna.'

'The first I knew of it, for certain, I mean, was when Guy came over here one night. We weren't expecting him—in fact we were getting ready for bed, it was after midnight. He was in a terrible state. Helen had been dead for a month or so. He'd been going through her belongings, he hadn't been able to make himself do it before then. He found a bundle of letters. I never saw them, Elaine, but Guy read every one. They were evidence of Helen's affair with a man who lives, or lived, in Cornwall. Truro, I believe. I think that's what Guy said. He—Guy hadn't had the faintest idea, you can imagine how stunned he was. The man was married and—well, that's it. That's about all I know.'

'You'd had an inkling, though. About the affair, I mean.'

Anna paled slightly. 'Yes, I—but that's all it was. I told you Helen and I were never close. I had nothing to go on except—what shall I call it? Women's intuition. I had only a suspicion, but I didn't *know* anything. Even if I had, there was nothing I could do; I could hardly have said anything to Guy, could I? That night he came here, well, it was obvious he'd had no idea about it.'

'But—but I don't understand it! Weren't they happy together? I've always thought——'

'They seemed to be, but who knows? As you said, one can't really know what goes on between people living together.'

Elaine was on her feet now, pacing around restlessly. 'Why didn't you tell me before. *Why?*'

'I've already explained that. I wanted to, but——'

'I'm sorry, that was unfair.' Elaine sat down again, her mind was spinning. 'Anna, would you make me a cup of coffee, please? I've got to think.' Think. Before she faced Guy. Think. This altered things drastically. But . . . She followed Anna in to the kitchen. 'But why was he jealous of *me*? Last night—Justin—surely he didn't suspect *me* of doing something underhand?'

Anna said nothing, she merely looked at her.

'Oh, God! It's ridiculous! Justin and I were flirting, that's all. I'm head over heels in love with my husband. I wouldn't——'

'But he doesn't know that, does he? You're right, you do need to think—carefully! Try to look at things from Guy's point of view. Think about that, for starters. You're considerably younger than he, you're extremely attractive, you married him under the guise of it being a 'sensible arrangement'—which he believed. You've never told him how much you care, so why shouldn't he suspect you of having an affair? Granted, he might have a certain paranoia about that sort of thing, but I don't think it's wholly unreasonable.'

Elaine did. It didn't wash with her. She had only to think of their lovemaking, their lovemaking as it had been in the beginning. People who were so physically content didn't go looking for affairs. No, Guy could not have seriously suspected her of it. Even more recently . . . right up until last night . . . their sex life had been more than satisfactory.

Hadn't it?

No. In a word, no! Hadn't she learned that there were many, many degrees of satisfaction, not all to do with the physical? One could satisfy hunger by the mechanical act of eating, eating anything . . . and still be left with a yearning for good flavour, something to savour.

In reality she couldn't, simply could *not* rule out the possibility of Guy having had his suspicions. *Having* suspicions. If that were the case, last night's flirtation with Justin would hardly have helped to dispel them! 'Oh, lord,' she murmured. 'Anna I've been such a fool!'

There was a kind smile. 'It's not too late. Cheer up.'

'I have to talk to him . . .'

'I've been telling you that for weeks. Sit down and have your coffee.'

Elaine sat, seeing the look of worry on the other woman's face. 'You're in a very awkward position, Anna, I realise that. Obviously I'd prefer to hear about this from Guy, but I can't get through to him at all, let alone with something like this. I can't see how I'm going to broach the subject.'

'It's all right. You can tell him you heard it from me. If he's furious with me, that's too bad. It'll be worth it.' Anna smiled, reached out a hand. 'Go home when you've finished your coffee, Elaine. We'll keep Jamie with us for the afternoon, to give you and Guy a chance to talk in private.'

'But he isn't in. I don't know where——'

'He isn't likely to stay out all day. He's probably doing some thinking of his own. I don't doubt he'll be back soon. So I'll drop Jamie off at—say, five o'clock. All right? And I won't come in, I'll just drop him on your doorstep. Now stop looking so worried. All you need to remember is that Guy loves you. He *does*, Elaine! Why else would he have reacted so jealously? You don't carry on like that with someone who means nothing to you.'

Elaine didn't say any more. She had never thought she meant nothing to Guy. But that was a long, long way from being loved. Anna's logic didn't compute as far as she was concerned; Guy might have reacted so angrily simply because he saw, thought he saw, history repeating itself. It might just be a case of the battered male ego. There was nothing at all which indicated he actually loved her.

CHAPTER ELEVEN

GUY wasn't back. Elaine got home just before two and the first thing she did was check the garage in case Guy had put his car away. It wasn't outside. It wasn't in the garage, either.

Where was he?

Not knowing what else she could do, she sat in the living room and waited. And waited. Three o'clock came and went.

Listlessly she got up, made a pot of coffee and drank several cups of it over the following, seemingly endless, hour. The soft chime of the carriage clock on the mantelpiece sounded loud in the still silence. Four o'clock. Elaine looked at the timepiece, which had been a wedding present. She closed her eyes, thinking about her wedding day, about their short honeymoon weekend which had been so full of passion and caring, of thoughtfulness on Guy's part.

. . . And then there had been the reality of driving down here on the Monday, of facing an uncertain future, adjusting to a new life, a new status. How right she had been to be nervous about it. How right she had been not to allow any illusions to start forming, to tell herself consciously to be wary of that.

If only she could know what was going through Guy's mind right now! He had said last night he had had as much as he could take. What had that meant, exactly? Enough of her, of this sham of a marriage? Maybe he wanted her to leave. Maybe talking would do no good at all. It might be too late for that.

Was it her fault? Partly. In spite of the sensible

166

warning she'd given herself, she had hoped for too much, too fast. Perhaps it was wholly her fault, perhaps living with her had been a disillusionment to Guy, not what he had expected, envisaged.

No, that didn't feel right. They had known enough about one another—in that respect, at least—to be sure, both of them, that they would be compatible. Compatible! Elaine laughed aloud. Hadn't she used that word when she had agreed to marry him, when she'd sought to justify her agreement with anything except the fact that she loved him and was in love with him? We're compatible, she had said, and I'm fond of you.

She got up again, wandered around the kitchen, poured herself a brandy she didn't drink and stood by the window in the living room. For a while she didn't think at all, she watched the rain trickling down the glass. Beyond the vast picture window she could see the sea, choppy, churning with white horses. The wind was getting stronger, turning the shower into a squall.

Then she burst into tears. The emotions, the fears churning inside her had become too much again. She sank on to a chair and cried until she was exhausted, her thoughts about Guy swinging back and forth like a pendulum. She grew angry, cursing him for staying out so long without so much as a word of warning.

Then the word *accident* sprang into her mind. Her anger vanished and was replaced by terror. What if he had had an accident? He drove that powerful car fast at the best of times—what sort of mood had he been in when he'd left the house this morning? And at what hour? It might have been the middle of the night for all she knew. Maybe he'd gone out immediately after he had . . . done what he did to her. In a rage. She had no way of knowing.

The clock chimed again. Again she looked at it, and was astonished to see it was not five but six o'clock.

Jamie! Anna had said she would bring Jamie home at five. Why hadn't she? Had the rain put her off or had Guy turned up there, perhaps?

She picked up the phone and dialled Anna's number. 'It's me. There's still no sign of Guy. He isn't there, is he?'

'Of course not. Are you okay?'

'Yes. I'm—I've been thinking. Nothing new particularly. It doesn't do much good.' Elaine sighed, resigning herself to more hours of waiting. 'You said you'd bring Jamie home. Shall I come and fetch him?'

'What?'

'I'll come for him if you like. I've nothing else to do and I don't see why you should come out in this weather. You've been kind enough as it is, keeping him——'

'Elaine, I dropped Jamie off an hour ago!' Anna did not hide her alarm. 'I didn't come in, I told you I wouldn't. I assumed Guy's car was in the garage and I thought it best—Elaine, I *saw* Jamie go into the house! I watched him go through the front door! He *must* be home.'

Elaine was on her feet, her eyes flitting around the room as if expecting to see her stepson. 'No!'

'He must be in his room, he must have gone straight upstairs.'

'Why should he? How——' A new wave of fear washed over her.

The suitcase. She had left her suitcase in the hall. She'd forgotten about it. And she had been crying. Jamie must have seen, heard ... 'Anna, I'm going to search the house.'

'Ring me back——' Anna began, but Elaine had already hung up.

She bolted upstairs. 'Jamie? Are you here, darling?' No answer. No sign. He wasn't in his room. She went as far as looking under the bed and in his wardrobe, in case he was hiding. Anna had seen him come into the house, he must have heard Elaine crying. What had he made of that? And the suitcase. Dammit, how stupid of her! She should have unpacked the thing, put it away, how could she have forgotten about it?

'Jamie?' He had run away. Even as she continued to search the house, the thought was forming. He was frightened, upset; he wasn't merely hiding—he had run away!

Less than five years old. He couldn't handle what he thought was happening. What was going through his mind? Where would a small child run to?

The woods.

Elaine raced to the downstairs cloakroom, pulled on a mac and flung open the kitchen door. She needed a torch—it was pitch dark out there. There was a powerful torch in the unit under the sink. She grabbed it and headed across the back lawn. The woods surrounded the house on three sides. On the south side of the house there was the sea. A long way down below the cliff, the rocks . . .

No! No, he wouldn't have gone in that direction. She wouldn't, couldn't, entertain the thought. The woods were far more intriguing to Jamie, thank heaven. He loved exploring in there, close to the house. He wouldn't have gone too far. If only it weren't so dark. 'Jamie? Jamie! Can you hear me, darling?' She skirted the outer perimeters, calling him over and over. Her raincoat snagged on something, stopping her in her tracks, causing her to drop the torch. Impatiently she unhooked herself, buttoned the coat up properly to stop it flapping in the wind. Brushing back her drenched hair, she groped for the torch and set off again.

A while later she moved deeper, back-tracking around the circle, calling his name frantically now. She stopped, listening hard for a sound, a response. There was nothing, nothing but the noise of the wind in the trees.

She needed help. She didn't dare go any deeper in case she got lost. If Jamie were deep in the woods he would be completely disorientated. Best get help. Quickly.

Elaine was disorientated herself. It took her a while to reach the edge of the woods, to see the lights from the house. As she ran across the long lawn at the back, the wind was so strong coming off the sea, it was all she could do to keep her balance.

She could hear the telephone shrilling as she approached the kitchen. It stopped just as she reached for it. 'Damn!' She snatched up the receiver and started dialling. It must have been Anna, wondering what was happening. She should have phoned her back first, before taking off for the woods, should have asked *then* for help.

'Elaine? *Elaine!*' It was Guy's voice, coming from the front of the house.

She dropped the receiver back on its cradle, unable to move for a moment. Guy's voice. Guy's voice with fear in it—unmistakable fear!

Elaine ran towards the hall and stopped dead as her eyes alighted on her husband. He looked grey, years older than he had when she had last seen him.

Jamie! The word echoed inside her head but she couldn't get it past her lips. It was stuck in her throat. Jamie! She'd been out ages, what had happened during that time? Had Jamie been found somewhere else while she'd been searching in the woods? A mental picture of the sea crashing against the rocks sprang in to her mind and she slumped against the wall, staring at Jamie's father, terrified by what he might tell her.

Guy was standing stock still, returning her stare. He was hunched forward as if he too were having trouble standing. Very quietly, helplessly, he said, 'Elaine, what are we going to do?'

She moved like lightning then, emitting a cry which

was almost a scream. She grabbed hold of Guy by the lapels of his coat. 'What do you *mean*?' she demanded. 'What do you *mean*? Have you found him? Where *is* he?'

He had no idea what she was talking about. It was obvious. He didn't need to say anything. He was looking at her as if she'd gone crazy. Elaine started talking, fast. Short, sharp sentences came tumbling out and formed a heap of disjointed information. 'Anna brought him home at five, but he didn't come in. I was crying and he probably heard me. I rang and said I'd go for him. I searched the house, but he isn't here, and I should have phoned her back and asked for help, but I belted out to the woods because I was convinced he'd be hiding there and——'

'*Stop!*' Guy was shaking her. Whatever had held him motionless had been forgotten. 'For heaven's sake, make sense. Now tell me, slowly, what's going on?'

'There's no time for that! Jamie's *missing*!'

'I've gathered that!' he barked. His hands clamped on to her shoulders. To her intense frustration he made her tell her story from the top. He listened, nodded, and seemed not unduly perturbed when she'd finished, except that he looked even greyer. 'Have you looked in the garden shed?' he asked calmly.

'No. I didn't think—but he never goes in there!'

'He might. He's little, but he's not stupid, is he? I can't imagine him hiding outside in this weather!'

No, Jamie wasn't stupid, he was far from that. But he was frightened and very, very upset. In his mind his world was falling to pieces. Just as he had suspected it would for a long time. 'I'll come with you.'

Guy was already on the move. 'No, it doesn't need two of us. Call Anna and put her in the picture; she must be frantic. Keep her on the line till I get back. If Jamie isn't hiding in the shed, we'll get Paul over.'

Paul was already over. There was the sound of the

front door closing, his voice calling out to them.

'In here,' Guy answered, just as the phone started ringing. He looked from his wife to the phone to Paul. 'Answer it,' he said to no one in particular.

Paul was about to follow him outside, but Elaine put a restraining hand on his arm. 'Hang on.' She picked up the phone and spoke to Anna. By the time she'd finished, Guy was back.

'No sign.'

Elaine relayed this to Anna. 'He's not in the shed. Have you got any ideas?'

'The garages,' Paul said. 'Have you checked there?'

Guy looked to Elaine. She shook her head, told Anna they were going to check the garages and that she'd ring back with a report.

All three of them trooped outside. They found Jamie in the second garage, in the darkness, huddled in the far corner. He recoiled as they approached, flinching against the light Guy switched on.

Elaine bit hard into her lip, dug her nails into her palms in an effort not to cry out. Her relief was such that she could have been sick, her reaction to the way Jamie recoiled one of self-loathing. She wouldn't forgive herself for this in a hurry.

'Come on, son,' Guy gathered him into his arms, talking quickly but softly. 'Everything's all right. There's no need to hide any more. Elaine's here, I'm here, and everything's all right. See?'

He carried Jamie to where Elaine was standing. She found herself being watched by two pairs of eyes, both grey and beautiful and . . . pleading. Had Paul's arm not slid tightly around her shoulders, she might not have found the strength to say the right thing. But she did. Precisely the right thing. 'Of course everything's all right! You had us all worried, darling,' she added, holding out her arms.

Guy handed him over. Jamie wrapped his arms around her neck in a stranglehold. He wasn't crying, but he sounded so weary it broke her heart. 'You were going to leave, though, weren't you?' He released her, pulling away so he could see her face. 'I saw your case! I knew you were leaving. That's why I had to hide. I waited behind the door till Anna went away and then I hid because I didn't want to see you go!'

So he hadn't actually heard her crying. If he had stayed behind the front door, he wouldn't have. She didn't know what to say. Neither, it seemed, did Guy. He too was looking at her, looking as lost as Jamie.

Paul knew what to say. 'Case?' he said casually. 'Do you mean the one in the hall, Jamie? The one with the dry-cleaning in it?'

Jamie's mouth fell open. Then he looked dubious. 'That's right,' Elaine plunged in. 'Is that what you meant, Jamie?'

He nodded, the dubiousness coming and going. 'Why, you goose!' she went on, 'I put lots of my summer clothes in there to get them cleaned for our holidays!'

It worked. The air tickets for their trip to Florida had arrived only the previous morning and Jamie had seen them. He knew they were leaving at the end of the month, just before Easter.

'I know you think our trip is a long way away, but it isn't. It's only three weeks. We have to start getting ready in good time, don't we? Which reminds me . . .' She went on as they walked back to the house, chatting, talking about shopping, buying him new things for his holiday. When he told her he was hungry, she knew all was well again.

All was well again . . . as far as Jamie was concerned.

She handed him over to Guy. 'A hot bath, then clean pyjamas for one very hungry young man, if you please. I'll get on with dinner.' Guy took hold of his son's hand, cast a look of gratitude in Paul's direction. 'Thanks, Paul. I'm sorry you and Anna were alarmed.'

'Forget it.' Paul waited until he was alone with Elaine before saying anything else. 'I'll push off now, but why don't I get you a brandy first? You look fit to drop.'

She nodded gratefully, sat on a kitchen stool and dropped her head in her hands. She didn't cry again. There were no more tears. There was only gratitude and regret and . . . and the hope that she might, just might, get through to her husband as she should have attempted to a long time ago.

CHAPTER TWELVE

THE three of them ate in the kitchen. Jamie's eyelids were drooping before he had finished his food. Together Elaine and Guy put him to bed, staying with him until he was asleep. Together they walked downstairs to the lounge. Then they were no longer together . . . they were merely in the same room.

Elaine sat, tongue-tied now they were alone. The atmosphere had changed, had become charged with tension in their sudden silence. It wasn't that she didn't know what to say, it was the difficulty of knowing where to start. Beyond their silence the rain was still belting against the windows, the wind moaning in fits and starts.

It was Guy who spoke first. He had been standing by the fireplace, his back to her. He reached for a cigarette, turning to face her but not able to meet her eyes. 'Elaine, about last night, I—an apology hardly seems adequate.'

'It is,' she said softly, able to be generous because now, at least, she knew what had motivated it, understood why he'd been angry. 'Your anger was misplaced, but——'

'You were leaving me, weren't you?'

'Yes. Yes, I was.' There was no point in trying to deny it now. 'I packed this morning. I came looking for you, to tell you.'

'What happened to change your mind?'

'Two things. Firstly I——' She couldn't get any further. It was she who was unable to meet his eyes now. She was going to say it, she *had* to say it, but she was afraid none the less of his reaction. She looked down at the carpet. 'Firstly, I love you. I can't leave you. You'd have to throw me out.'

Silence again.

When it became unbearable Elaine looked up at him, her eyes frantic although she didn't realise it. Guy was staring at her, unable to believe what he'd heard. 'Dear God,' he murmured, 'if only you knew how much I've wanted to hear you say that!'

'Guy, we must——'

'Say it again,' he demanded. 'Let me hear you say it again!'

'I love you. I've always loved you. I loved you before I married you but I didn't want to give you the onus of knowing it.'

'Onus? *Onus?*' He hadn't moved, he was still standing by the fireplace, clearly in a state of shock. 'Elaine, what on earth is that supposed to mean?'

Again she had to look away. 'I mean the responsibility, the burden of knowing, knowing and being unable to return my love. And I—I thought you might think me foolish. Considering what I'd told you, my theories about marriage, I thought——'

He was laughing. There was no amusement in it, just irony.

Elaine's heart was in her throat. 'Guy, please! I don't see——'

'No.' The laughter stopped. 'There's a great deal you don't see, which is my fault entirely. Oh, Elaine, stop looking at me like that! I love you too, don't you know it?'

'N-no! How—why——'

'Why should you? How could you? After last night I can understand that.'

She was on her feet, excited, frightened, frustrated. All of those. 'It has nothing to do with last night's incident. *Forget* that. Stop worrying about it. Guy, don't you realise I've believed all this time that you were still in love with Helen?'

'For heaven's sake!'

'It's true! And why not? How was I to know what your life with her was really like? I still don't. All I know is that she was unfaithful to you. I don't know *why*, I don't know how you felt about it.'

'Anna, I presume? She told you.'

'Yes. When I told her I was leaving you. I—went over there this morning to collect Jamie. I was going to bring him home and wait for you to come back. I was going to explain everything—try to explain everything—to him.'

They were still apart. They were communicating at last, but there was still so much Elaine needed to hear before she could believe there was a chance at real happiness. 'Why don't you tell me about it, Guy?'

He came over to her then. He took both her hands in his and led her to the settee. 'Sit down, darling. I'm about to do just that. I should have told you about it right from the beginning, before we married, but it didn't seem relevant. I mean it, it really didn't. I'd got over it, over Helen's death and everything else, long since. There was no reason I should have suspected this of coming between us, changing things between us. Besides,' he added quietly, 'it isn't something I'm proud of, exactly.'

Elaine's eyes closed. 'Oh, Guy! Hold me, just hold me for a moment. I've been so afraid!'

He held her, tightly, stroking the black silk of her hair in the way he always used to. 'So have I. I'm not about to lie to you, Elaine. I don't think I loved you when I married you, at least I didn't realise it if I did. I can't say when it happened, at what point I started to love you, but I can tell you when it hit me, what day it was. It was that day we had the fight in January, when you'd been out shopping.'

He held her away from him, his eyes beseeching for understanding. 'I came home early, the house was empty. The silence seemed—it's hard to explain. I—walking into an empty house when I'd expected to find you . . .'

He shrugged. Guy Harris, normally so fluent with words, was having difficulty expressing himself! 'I realised then, at that precise moment, that I loved you. Only then. As I say, I can't tell you when it happened but that was when I acknowledged it. I'm not proud of the way I treated you when you got home, Elaine, I hope you believe me.'

He moved away, was on his feet again and shifting restlessly, his fingers shoving his still damp hair back from his face. 'While I was waiting for you I had all sorts of crazy ideas. They got out of proportion. Firstly I thought you might have left, that you wouldn't be coming back at all. I know,' he held up a hand, his look apologetic now. 'I know that was ridiculous. I knew it then. I dismissed it. But I couldn't dismiss the rest of it. That's when I got you and Helen mixed up. You see, I—was reminded of her. There were times with Helen when I found myself in a similar situation, me at home while she was out. I never suspected she was seeing someone, can you credit that? She would come home behaving perfectly naturally, always telling me where she'd been. And I always believed her.'

He broke off, sighing deeply. 'My stupidity gets worse. A few months before she got pregnant, she asked me for a divorce.'

Elaine looked at him blankly. Anna hadn't mentioned this, so she couldn't have known about it. 'A divorce? So things were bad between you.'

'No.' Guy smiled, a wry smile. 'That's the madness of it. Things weren't bad. Or so I thought. It came out of the blue: I was pole-axed. I didn't think she meant it at first—I thought she was joking. When it became clear she wasn't, I asked what was wrong. I didn't know, had never thought for a moment that anything was wrong!'

'And?'

'She said she was bored. Plain and simple. Bored, bored, bored! I quote.'

'She didn't tell you then that she was seeing someone else?'

'Not even a hint of it.'

Elaine was confused. 'I'm having trouble understanding the woman. Surely it would have been healthier to tell you the truth, no matter how it would hurt?'

Guy seemed genuinely amused at that. 'It would have been more honest, I don't know about healthier—from her point of view, I mean. After she died, when I learned the truth, I could reach only two conclusions. I still don't know which is the right one. Either she still loved me to some extent, and didn't really want a divorce, or it was simply more convenient to stay with me. The man she was having an affair with was married, living not too far away, in the Truro area. I found his letters to her after she died, one night when I was going through her things.'

'Where were they sent to? Not here, surely?'

'Oh, no.' There was a hint of bitterness now. He was entitled to it. 'Helen was more devious than that—she wasn't stupid. They were sent care of a post office box number. It seemed that every time they got together, he sent her a letter afterwards. He made it very plain to Helen that he wouldn't divorce his wife. He said he loved her but he wouldn't break up his home for her. He had two children and I have to say this much for him, he was honest with her. From what I could gather he was some sort of executive who could get away from home often, easily. Maybe the company he worked for, or owned, had a branch down here. I just don't know. What I do know is that the affair had been going on for more than two years, that when I was away Helen spent nights with him in some small hotel whose name was never mentioned in the letters. By the time I learned all this, it was hardly relevant. Nevertheless it was a terrible blow, a total shock. I've no idea where or when she met the man, or who he is. The letters were signed Douglas. Some of them were . . . well, let's say I regretted reading them.'

Elaine groaned inwardly. She was still at a loss to understand his first wife. 'Guy, I hope you never doubted for a moment that Jamie is your child. You've only to look at him——'

'No. He's a carbon copy of me, heaven help him. Besides, he was conceived while Helen and I were abroad. After her announcement about wanting a divorce, we talked. Not at any length. Her complaint, she said, was simple boredom. I blamed myself for it. I had thought her resourceful, had never dreamt she was bored. Since then I've wondered—well, if we'd had a child earlier, as we'd wanted, this affair might never have started. I've also wondered whether I neglected her.'

'But she knew what she was in for when you married, didn't she? You were already an established writer, she must have known how much your career meant to you, that she'd be left alone when you were working.'

'Yes, she knew all that,' he shrugged. 'Anyhow, I tried to spend more time with her from then on. We took a month's vacation in Hawaii before moving on to Florida for the winter. For me that trip was like a second honeymoon.' Guy caught the look on Elaine's face, it wasn't hard to read her mind. 'No,' he said bluntly, 'there was nothing wrong with our sex life, either, which is something else that made her affair difficult to understand.' He paused, watching her. 'Note the past tense, Elaine. Made it difficult to understand *at the time*. Sex with Helen was always good but it was nothing compared to what we have, you and I. I'd had plenty of women before I married, but I've never known a lover as exciting as you. I can only assume, now, that what Helen had with Douglas was similiar to what you and I have.'

'That's my guess, too. Once you've experienced that sort of sexual compatibility—well, I should imagine it's hard to settle for less. But go on, Guy, Helen got pregnant while you were on holiday?'

'Yes. I was delighted, we both were. We'd planned to have a bunch of kids, but——' He broke off, sighing. 'We only think we can plan our lives, Elaine. Sometimes something else steps in, God, Fate, call it what you will. Still, I thought our problem, or rather Helen's problem, was solved. I thought she'd be happier, more content with a baby to look after. Goddammit, Elaine!' He exploded suddenly, making her jump. 'She *seemed* to be, but she still saw Douglas *after* Jamie was born! He was born in June, the last letter I found from Douglas was dated September, just two months before she died.'

'I'm not sure why you're so angry,' Elaine said quietly. 'Hurt pride, perhaps?'

'Partly. I'm human. But there's much more than that. I was angry at my own stupidity, blindness. I should have suspected something, but I didn't. Maybe that's due to some incredible arrogance on my part.'

Elaine smiled. 'Take it easy. You said yourself Helen was devious about things. She never intended you to find out, even when she asked you for a divorce. My own opinion is that she did love you, Guy. Not madly, as she had when you married, when she was years younger. She had probably grown into a different person with different needs. And as we've agreed, we can't overlook the physical side of things. I have to say it, I think if Douglas had been prepared to divorce, to marry Helen, she'd have left you all right. But she'd have done it with the minimum of hurt, because she loved you, too. I'm convinced of that. Her love had merely changed its form, its intensity. As things turned out, Jamie came along and—and who's to say what would have happened, had she lived?'

She got up to pour herself a drink. 'What I want to know is how your mind was working that day in January when we fought. You can't seriously have suspected me of being with someone else.'

'No. Intellectually, no. Emotionally . . . a great deal was resurrected during the couple of hours I was waiting for you. Four years ago, after Helen died and I learned the truth about her, I did a lot of thinking. You can imagine. Looking back I saw a pattern to her behaviour over the previous couple of years. Her routine had changed insidiously. Where once she would go out with her mother or with girl friends, she started going out alone. Shopping, she said, or riding, walking. Solitary occupations.

'Suffice it to say I was so damned insecure about you that when I came home unexpectedly and found you not in, I suspected you immediately . . . sort of. I mean——'

Elaine sighed, nodding sadly. 'I understand, Guy. You mean you did and you didn't. But *why* were you so insecure about me? There was absolutely no need——' Her voice trailed off. She already knew the answer to that. She had never told him how much she cared. They had been married a month at the time, he could easily have thought her disillusioned. Indeed, he had asked her the following day whether she thought she'd made a mistake. 'We should have talked,' she said wearily. 'It wasn't enough that we asked one another if we'd made a mistake, we should have talked things through thoroughly.'

'We tried——'

'No, we didn't! Because we were both scared, scared of what we might learn, hear. Oh, Guy, we've been so stupid! Nothing was the same after that awful day. Our relationship has been deteriorating ever since!'

'It's my fault.'

'*No!* I won't accept that! You think you were insecure? It was far worse for me! I was busy assuming everyone was comparing me with Helen, when actually it was *I* who was doing that! Darling, I've been convinced you were still in love with her, with the memory of her.'

'The memory of her? My God! The memory of her was sullied the day I discovered the truth. I resented her deception. I hated it and I resented it. I'd rather have known the truth at *any* cost. Here . . .' He took the glass from her hand. 'Let me get you a refill—I could use a drink myself.'

'Sorry.' She smiled guiltily, she hadn't thought to pour him a drink when she'd got hers. 'I didn't think——'

'That's the trouble, Elaine. Neither of us has been thinking straight.'

It was true. Oh, how very true it was! 'Guy, you never told Esther and Edward about Helen's affair, did you?'

'No. What point? I confess there were moments when I wanted to, shortly after her death, when Esther would weep and go on about what a good, perfect girl she was. She'd talk about her for hours at a stretch. But I couldn't do it. We human beings protect each other in strange ways sometimes. I couldn't disillusion Esther.'

Protect each other. Elaine thought about that. Helen had protected Guy from the truth, he had protected her parents, and she herself had . . . 'I've been doing that with you. I've come to the conclusion it's not always a good thing.'

'What? You mean by not letting me know how you feel about me?' Guy sat beside her now, putting their drinks on a coffee table. He took hold of her hand, held it to his lips and kissed each fingertip.

She looked at him directly. 'Not only that. I never told you how much it's bothered me when Esther mentioned Helen's name to me. I've hated it. I understood it, but I've hated it. And—and I never told you because I didn't want you to know that . . . that I was jealous.'

'Elaine! Silly darling . . .' Guy reached for her, held her gently against him in the circle of his arms. 'There's something I have to add,' she went on. 'It's important. I want you to understand that Esther's words will never affect me again, Guy. They can't now I know you love me.'

His arms tightened around her, but she pulled away so she could look at him, see his eyes. 'But they did because I've been so insecure. And that changed me, I know it did. As time passed I got more and more uptight, more demanding. I wanted you to love me as I love you. I know it changed my attitude towards you; at first I resented the situation, then I began to resent you because I loved you so much, if that makes sense. It's part of the reason we grew so distant. So don't blame yourself for all this, not wholly. It would have been better to tell me everything months ago, I agree, but you didn't, so that's that. But I've handled things badly, too. I've been jealous, jealous of what I believed to be an ideal marriage.'

'I'm not sure there's any such thing.' He smiled, taking hold of her again, adding softly, 'But I think ours will get very, very close to it. I love you, Elaine, I love you very much. I hate to think of the time we've wasted, the way we've been hurting each another. Last night when I saw you flirting with that—that self-opinionated Galsworthy, it triggered a fury in me I didn't know I was capable of. I wanted to strangle him and I wanted to punish you even while I knew there was nothing to it. I feared there might be in the future. Things were so bad between us, I couldn't be sure you wouldn't look elsewhere. And he's a very attractive man.'

'Not to me. Handsome, yes, attractive no. I don't even like him. Oh, Guy, I'm sorry! I don't know what I was thinking about last night.'

'We mustn't hurt each other again, darling. We mustn't ever let anything like that happen again. Promise me you'll be honest with me, no matter what.'

'I will! I will, I swear it!'

Guy caught hold of her chin, looked deeply into her

eyes. 'No more misunderstandings, starting now. You do love me, don't you?'

'Yes! Oh, God, yes!'

'And you're not bored, living here?'

His question alarmed her, brought tears to her eyes. Guy had been damaged more than he realised by his discovery about Helen. It was hardly surprising. The disillusionment had been enormous. To believe all is well in one's life and then to discover that the truth is very different must lead to doubts about reality from then on. He needed reassurance, more than she had given him so far.

'Listen,' she said gently, 'and think about this carefully. I'm twenty-three, the same age Helen was when you married her. But I'm *different*, Guy. I, too, will change over the coming years. Naturally. Everyone changes. But I began my marriage to you in a different position from Helen, from a different starting point. You knew before you married me what kind of life I like. I've been something of a drop-out, I went after and established a quiet life-style that suits me totally and——' She broke off, smiling at him. 'I hate to say it, but we're *compatible*. We *are*! Unlike Helen I have my work, work I adore. You and I both love what we do, we understand one another's obsessions, we don't interfere or demand or resent it if we're left alone. To use a phrase you're fond of: we respect it.'

Her smile faded, was replaced by a look of sadness. 'I hate to say this, too, when Jamie is Helen's son, the child she hardly knew. But—I have a ready-made family, there's no room in my life for boredom.'

Guy was grinning, pulling her against him, his lips seeking hers. 'In fact you're going to be a very busy lady, because if I have anything to do with it, we'll have another half dozen children.'

Elaine giggled at that. 'Six? Well, perhaps two . . . or

three. And that,' she added, kissing him lightly, teasingly, 'brings me to the last point I was going to make. There's this.' She slid her hands beneath his sweater, letting her fingers trail along the hard muscles of his back. 'We have this, too. Something quite, quite extraordinary.'

Which it was. When Guy kissed her in earnest she knew without doubt that what they'd had before, they had again. And there was more, even more . . .

Elaine learned of yet another dimension to lovemaking when Guy led her upstairs to their bed, when he started to undress her, caress her. It was better, even better, knowing he loved her. They were together now, together as they had been before, transported to a land of pure sensuality, at one with each other.

Hours later when finally they were ready to sleep, when they were wrapped in each other's arms, he teased her about the theories she had once expounded. 'Well, Mrs Harris? Would you still say that love isn't an essential ingredient for a happy marriage?'

'Yes,' she murmured. It was all she could do to answer him, she was so sleepy. 'I maintain that it isn't. But experience has taught me I have to qualify that statement, so let me say it isn't essential provided both people feel the same. It's very awkward indeed if there's an imbalance, if one loves and the other doesn't.'

'Or if that appears to be the case.'

'Or if that appears to be the case.' Elaine cuddled closer, her eyes closing of their own volition. She couldn't talk any more but she would tell him, tomorrow, that it did make things a whole lot nicer when love was present, a whole lot nicer.

Tomorrow . . . She drifted to sleep thinking about all their tomorrows, in Cornwall or in Florida, or possibly in California. It didn't matter to either of them. What mattered was that they were together. Their relationship had undergone another change. The difference was that they were together now in spirit, in body and in mind.

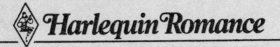
Harlequin Romance

Coming Next Month

Available in October wherever paperback books are sold, or
through Harlequin Reader Service.

In the U.S.
901 Fuhrmann Blvd.
P.O. Box 1397
Buffalo, N.Y. 14240-1397

In Canada
P.O. Box 603
Fort Erie, Ontario
L2A 5X3

**For the millions who can't read
Give the Gift of Literacy**

One out of five adults in North America
cannot read or write well enough
to fill out a job application
or understand the directions on a bottle of medicine.

**You can change all this by joining the fight
against illiteracy.**

For more information write to:
Contact, Box 81826, Lincoln, Neb. 68501
In the United States, call toll free: 1-800-228-8813

**The only degree you need
is a degree of caring**

**It was a misunderstanding that could cost a young woman her
virtue, and a notorious rake his heart.**

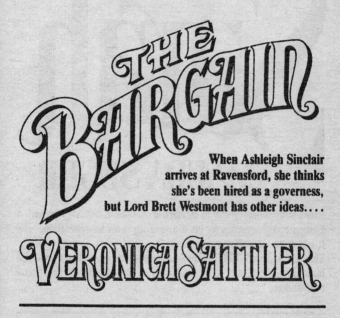

When Ashleigh Sinclair
arrives at Ravensford, she thinks
she's been hired as a governess,
but Lord Brett Westmont has other ideas....

Sarah

MAURA SEGER

Sarah wanted desperately to escape the clutches of her cruel father.
Philip needed a mother for his son, a mistress for his plantation.
It was a marriage of convenience.
Then it happened. The love they had tried to deny suddenly became a
blissful reality... only to be challenged by life's hardships and brutal
misfortunes.

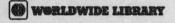